His eyes were [...]
with a silent plea

"Sanny," Mark began in a cool, low voice, "one night I'm holding a warm, willing woman in my arms, and the next she won't even talk to me. Am I not supposed to be bothered by that? I didn't come with you to Accra just for a little nocturnal bliss."

"You're lucky you got it anyway," Sanny replied. Her legs were trembling. She was losing her sanity, saying all the wrong things.

His face grew taut. "I didn't force you."

"I'm not blaming you," she insisted. "Please let me go...."

"I can't," he said, and the odd, husky note in his voice surprised her. With a groan, he pulled her to him, kissing her with a wild, impatient fierceness that shocked her into surrender.

Books by Karen van der Zee

KAREN
VAN DER ZEE

one more time

Harlequin Books

TORONTO • NEW YORK • LONDON
AMSTERDAM • PARIS • SYDNEY • HAMBURG
STOCKHOLM • ATHENS • TOKYO • MILAN

Harlequin Presents first edition May 1984
ISBN 0-373-10694-7

Original hardcover edition published in 1983
by Mills & Boon Limited

CHAPTER ONE

'Am I in your way?' Drink in hand, the tall man stood leaning against the doorpost, effectively blocking her passage as well as that of everyone else at the party.

'Yes,' she said, 'but what the heck.'

He grinned. 'Were you leaving?' His teeth were very white, his eyes a bright blue in the tanned face.

'No. I was trying to find the kitchen.'

'I see.' It was obvious that he didn't. 'May I get you a drink?'

'Please.' The air was heavy with cigarette smoke, perfume, alcohol. People were laughing and talking, drinking whisky sodas, Martinis, gin and tonics. 'Milk, please,' she said.

His face showed no reaction, only in the depth of the blue eyes did she catch a flicker of disbelief.

'Right,' he said, 'this way.'

In the kitchen he opened the refrigerator and examined the contents. Sitting on a stool, Sanny watched him as he took out a pitcher of milk and poured some in a glass.

'You've got to be kidding,' he said as he handed it to her. 'How can you drink this reconstituted stuff?' His face registered great distaste.

She shrugged lightly. 'What choice do I have? No cows, no milk. It's better than nothing.' She drank the milk. It wasn't very good, but in the two months she'd been in West Africa she'd become used to it.

The man had perched himself on top of the counter, long legs dangling. He was very good-looking in a funny sort of way—a little rough and unfinished. He was watching her, and she felt a small thrill of excitement.

'Ulcer?' he asked casually.

She frowned. 'What? Oh, no, I'm in excellent health, thank you.'

'Due to drinking milk rather than alcohol, no doubt. Do you smoke?'

'Only cigars.' She kept her face straight.

He laughed. 'You take vitamins?'

Sanny was starting to enjoy this. 'Geritol every day.'

'And you exercise, eat well and get eight hours of sleep every night.' He didn't miss a beat.

'Nine,' she corrected.

He looked at his watch. 'It's past your bedtime—I should probably take you home.'

It couldn't be more than ten. 'Sometimes I stay up late . . . depending.'

'Depending on what?'

She gave him a saintly smile. 'Oh, different things.'

'I won't touch that one.' There was laughter in his eyes.

'No, better not.'

'Have you had dinner yet?' he asked.

She nodded. 'Of course. Soy-bean soup and bean-sprout salad.'

'Ah, a vegetarian.'

'A vegan,' she amended.

His eyes lingered meaningfully on the now empty glass of milk. Then his gaze came back to her face. 'If I'm not mistaken, vegans do not ingest any food of animal origin, including eggs, cheese, milk . . .'

Sanny grinned. 'Well, sometimes I sin.'

The corner of his mouth turned up in a crooked smile. 'Well, don't we all,' he commented dubiously. 'Would you like to go back to that riot of fun?' He made a vague gesture in the direction of the living room where Liberians and Americans and other foreigners were playing the cocktail party game.

No. She might lose him in the crowd. 'I like the kitchen better—it's quiet.'

'And there's milk in the refrigerator.'

'That too.'

He looked at her speculatively. 'Actually, I'm going to have to find myself some dinner. I just flew in from Freetown and they didn't feed me on the plane. Would you care to join me?'

'You just came from Sierra Leone?' she asked. 'I was there for three weeks. I just came to Monrovia last week. Not by plane, though, I hitched down the coast.'

His eyebrows shot up. 'Good lord, you're a brave one. Powdered milk and hitching down the coast!'

'It's a lot more interesting than sitting on a plane with a bunch of boring businessmen and diplomats. I've got stories to tell.'

He nodded. 'I can imagine,' he said dryly. 'So why don't you come with me, have some dinner and tell me your stories?'

'I don't even know your name.' She gave him her most charming smile. Maybe he's one of those boring businessmen, she thought, though he didn't really look like one.

'Mark Taylor,' he replied solemnly. 'Professor of Social Economics on temporary assignment with the U.S. Information Service. And you?'

'Sanny.'

'Sanny what?'

'Sanny Joy Copeland, itinerant journalist.'

'Sanny Joy,' he repeated slowly, as if tasting the words. 'I like it.'

'I hate it. It sounds like the name of a toilet bowl cleaner.'

He roared, his head thrown back.

Let him laugh. Let him think it was a joke. There were a lot of things to hate her mother for. The hypocrisy of her name was only one of the minor ones.

'Well,' he said, 'I must say it didn't sound to me like that. And now that we've properly introduced ourselves, are you willing to brave dinner with me?'

Actually, she could use some food. She hadn't eaten dinner, thinking she could make do with the fancy little doodads passed around at the party, but she was still hungry. More important, it would be a shame to have Mark Taylor walk out of here by himself. She wouldn't mind some more of his company.

So she accepted his invitation. Did she know her way around Monrovia? he asked. Only a little, she said, but she wasn't familiar with any restaurants since she ate local food most of the time. It had taken courage and determination initially, but had proved to be a rewarding experience. Also, it made it possible to stay within her budget.

In the last couple of months she'd eaten a lot of fruit—pineapples, paw-paws, bananas, mangoes— purchased by the road or in village markets. Fruit was safe to eat. Meat and fish stews were usually cooked a long time and she hadn't had much trouble with her digestive tract. Water and fresh vegetables were to be avoided. She was always careful.

After being in the air-conditioned coolness of the house, walking out into the dark, humid night was like entering a Turkish steam bath. They were in a quiet residential area with large, beautiful houses owned or rented by businessmen, government officials and foreign nationals. The houses were surrounded by extensive gardens with tall palms and flowering tropical bushes.

'We'll catch a cab at the main road,' he said. 'Do you mind a short stroll?'

'Not at all.' He should have seen some of the 'strolls' she'd taken in the last weeks! Her sandals were comfortable enough, the long, wide cotton dress with

its elaborate African embroidery was easy to move in.
She'd bought the dress in Senegal. It was made of a
colourful African print and was easily washed and
ironed. She could wear it to parties, dinners, anywhere
after dark. She'd brought with her two pairs of
sandals, a few cotton dresses, a pair of jeans and a
couple of shirts. Heaviest of all were her notebooks
and files filled with her travel experiences, thoughts
and ideas.

It didn't take long for a taxi to materialise.

'Charter,' Mark Taylor said to the driver, indicating
that he wanted the taxi for himself and not to stop and
pick up other passengers as well. 'The Hotel Dukor,
please.'

'Is that where you're staying?' Sanny asked. He was
one of the lucky ones, staying in a good hotel.

He nodded. 'The restaurant is one of the best in
town. Where are you staying?'

'The Arrivederci.' A very appropriate name, but
why Italian, she had no idea.

'Never heard of it.'

'That's good.' She grinned, seeing his eyebrows rise
at her dry reply.

'Oh?'

'Not first rate. At night it's a hang-out for ladies of
the night. I have to battle my way through the lobby
with every male in the place looking me over. It was
very disconcerting at first.' Her voice was bland.

'But it doesn't bother you any more?'

'Oh, no, not at all,' she said lightly, 'apart from the
fact that it makes me feel like a piece of meat.'

'My God, why do you stay in a place like that?' he
exclaimed.

'It's cheap. And my room isn't bad. Besides, the
place looked perfectly respectable at noon when I
registered.'

'Who sent you out here? Don't they pay you?'

'Nobody sent me out here. I came on my own.'

He gave her a long look, but said nothing. The taxi driver turned on his radio and the rhythmic beat of some popular African Highlife song filled the car. The driver hummed along, turning a corner at too high a speed, and Sanny was thrown sideways against Mark Taylor's shoulder.

'Sorry,' she muttered, straightening.

'My pleasure.' There was humour in his voice. 'Here we are.'

She wouldn't mind staying in a nice hotel like this for a change, Sanny thought as they walked through the spacious lobby to the restaurant.

'I know you said you'd had dinner already,' Mark commented as they were seated, 'but if you're hungry again, feel free.' He handed her the menu. 'I don't know what there is for vegans.' He looked down the list. 'I think I'll have a steak myself.'

A steak. Boy, would she like a steak!

'I'll have the same,' she said.

He looked up without surprise. 'Not a vegan after all. I didn't think so. Wine?'

She grinned. 'I would love some wine.'

'Don't tell me,' he said, watching her eat, 'that this is your first meal of the day.'

'I won't—it's not. But this is wonderful. I haven't had a good steak for a long time. As I said, I eat local food, mostly.'

'Because it's cheap?'

'And because it's more interesting. I mean, I have stories to tell. . . .'

He nodded. 'Right. You have stories to tell.' He chewed on a piece of steak, examining her critically. 'Why are you here?'

'In Africa, you mean?'

'Yes. You said nobody sent you.'

'I sent myself,' she explained. 'It was in my

horoscope, you see. I was getting bored with my job. I worked for a city newspaper for three years and I was tired of doing the same thing over and over and I wasn't getting anywhere.' She paused briefly and took a sip of her wine. 'One day I bought one of those paperback horoscope books that tell you all about what's in store for you in the next year. It said that there were great prospects for exotic foreign travel, that I would encounter promising career challenges, and that I should give in uninhibitedly to my wanderlust fantasies. So here I am.' She smiled at him serenely.

'Fascinating.' His face was carefully expressionless, but the blue eyes held laughter. 'So why Africa? Why not Guadeloupe or Singapore or the Amazon? Or was that in the horoscope too?'

'No, it didn't specify, so I started looking for signs and omens—you know what I mean. First person I talked to after I'd read the book was an old lady I met on a bus, and she started telling me all about her grandson who worked in Africa and was having all sorts of exciting adventures, so I knew it had to be Africa. But by the time I got home I couldn't remember where in Africa this guy was—my geography was never very good, you know. So, anyway, next day at the paper I found a wall map—my editor had a huge one in his office—and I closed my eyes and aimed my finger in the general direction of Africa and it landed in the Atlantic Ocean just off the coast of Senegal, so I figured that's where I should start.'

She was making it all up as she went along—the horoscope, the lady on the bus, and the map on the wall, and she was enjoying herself thoroughly. She offered him an angelic smile and he looked at her with remote amusement, taking a leisurely sip of his wine.

'I don't suppose,' he said evenly, 'you've ever heard of self-fulfilling prophecies.'

She shook her head, making her eyes wide and innocent. 'No. What's that?'

'Remind me to tell you some time.'

Sanny smiled sunnily. 'I'll do that . . . some time.'

'It's a deal.'

She speared a piece of steak on her fork. She liked him. Nice man. Probably didn't believe a word she had told him, which was just as well.

She'd come to Africa because the place had fascinated her for a very long time and the reason why she couldn't even remember. She'd felt stuck and stranded at the *Chronicle*, reporting on local affairs, and she'd decided one sunny spring day that enough was enough. She wanted to travel, do freelance writing, be independent. Having told her editor of her plans, she had left her job, but committed herself to writing a weekly column about her adventures for the paper's travel section. This was wonderful, as it would help her financial situation for the time being. She was not afraid of hard work, strange food and hot weather, but hunger was not among her many ambitions.

She wanted to write a book, a travelogue with a difference. She had all kinds of ideas that were taking shape now that she was travelling around West Africa. She was spending many a hot hour writing and revising, sitting under a mango tree, or at the beach, or in a dingy little hotel room.

'Where have you been so far?' Mark asked, having finished his food and pushing his chair back.

'After Senegal I went to Gambia, then Sierra Leone, and then I came here to Liberia.' She told him she'd flown from New York to Dakar, had landed at night, cleared Customs and Immigration, shared a taxi with someone she'd met on the plane and gone to a hotel. She'd been so terrified she hadn't moved out of the hotel for two days.

Apparently he found that amusing.

Everything had been so different, strange, frightening, somehow. She'd never been out of the country before, not even to Canada or Mexico. She couldn't make herself understood. The French that people spoke in Senegal didn't resemble the French she'd learned in college.

Realising she wasn't going to discover Africa by sitting in a hotel room, she had eventually gathered all her courage and ventured out into town. It had surprised her to see so many big Western-style buildings, to see men dressed in business suits as well as in more traditional garb. She'd discovered the city had everything—theatres and monuments and cafés and discos.

'They call Dakar the Paris of Africa, did you know that?' she asked.

He nodded. 'I did,' he acknowledged dryly. 'The President of Senegal is a poet. He's very interested in culture and the arts.'

'A poet? A real poet, you mean?'

'Very real.'

'Imagine that! A poet for president!' Over time the United States had been under the influence of lawyers and businessmen, and lately a peanut farmer and an actor. She wondered vaguely what the effect would be of having a poet in the White House. Maybe it was what the country needed.

Nice buildings and centres of cultural activity were not all that made up Dakar. Sanny had discovered slums and beggars and other depressing sights as well.

She'd been lucky to find a teenage boy who spoke an adequate amount of English. He was a handsome young man, his dark face intelligent and serious, his manner dignified and courteous, and he seemed too old for his age. He wanted to be a politician, he'd told her. He had travelled with her and helped her with her interviews. She wanted to talk to as many people as

she could, and he had been invaluable in those early
days. He had also started her off on the local diet of
rice and fish.

She told Mark about her trip to the pilgrimage town
of Touba and the mosque she had seen, about the days
she had spent in a fishing village watching the
hundreds of brightly painted pirogues come in with
their catch of tuna, and about the women on the beach
selling fish.

She could talk to him for another week about the
things she had seen and done, but she decided
somewhere between dessert and another glass of wine
that she'd better stop talking before he got tired of
listening.

'Coffee?' he asked, not really looking as if he was
tired of her voice.

'I'd love some. This was a great dinner, thanks.'

'You're quite welcome.' His eyes were dancing and
she felt suddenly uncomfortable, which was very
surprising, since she didn't feel uncomfortable with
men very often. She had no idea what was happening
to her. She looked away and watched the other diners
with feigned interest. There was something about this
man that began to make her feel slightly uneasy. It was
ridiculous. No man got to her like this. Was it his
eyes? The way he looked at her? She didn't know.

He had said very little all through dinner, just
letting her do the talking, which was surprising too,
since she was usually the one to listen—it was her job
to make people talk to her. Glancing back at the
strong, angular face, she wondered what kind of man
he was. A professor, he'd said. He didn't look like a
professor. He was young, in his early thirties, she
guessed, and he looked more the outdoorsy type. It
was hard to visualise him at a desk spending his hours
poring over tons of verbiage.

'Tell me what you're doing here,' she suggested,

reaching for the coffee that had been placed at her side.

'I'm on a lecture tour. Very uninteresting.'

'Oh, I don't believe that.' Nothing about this man could be uninteresting. 'Tell me about it.'

'If you insist. I'll try to make it entertaining.'

He really had an impossible grin. Sanny listened to him talk, filing away all the information in her memory. She watched him intently, which was the polite thing to do, but it also gave her the opportunity to examine his face a little better. She liked looking at him, seeing the expressions change on his face, seeing his white teeth when he grinned, the eyes light up when he laughed. She liked his hair, blond, smooth and straight, one lock flopping heavily across his forehead.

Later he took her back to her hotel in a rickety taxi with flowers painted on the doors and insisted gallantly on guiding her through the lobby to her room. The bar, which was off the lobby and in full view, was congested with people in search of a good time. Mark looked with amusement at the young women who eyed him up and down and threw angry glances at Sanny.

'They think you're my catch,' she said, 'and that I'm intruding on their territory.'

'There are several things I could say to that,' he said, 'but I won't.'

'Good.' She started climbing the stairs to the second floor. 'Listen, I'm okay. You don't need to take me up all the way.'

'I need the exercise.'

She stopped in front of her door and put the key in the lock. 'Thanks again for the dinner,' she said nicely, dismissing him. Why did she feel so uneasy? She held on to the unlocked door, not opening it. She wasn't going to invite him in.

His hand came down on her shoulder and she felt the heavy warmth through the thin cotton. His eyes were smiling when she looked at him. Was he laughing at her?

'See you soon,' he said softly, leaning forward and brushing her lips with his. 'Sleep well.' He turned and was gone.

Sanny went into the room and got ready for bed. She was wide awake. Maybe she should work for a while, type out the notes she'd made today. She had rented a small typewriter which was sitting on a wobbly table provided by the hotel. The legs were uneven and she had had to fold up a piece of newspaper to place under one leg and even them out.

She sat down with a sigh and stared at the notebook full of her scribbles. Okay, let's get going, she admonished herself, picking up a sheet of typing paper and rolling it in the machine.

She worked for about half an hour, at first aware of music and laughter and other noises of merriment coming up from other parts of the hotel, but tuning them out after a while. Then the buzzing of a mosquito began to irritate her. It flew around her head and face and she swiped at it a few times without success. Scraping back the chair, she got up, found a copy of *Drum Magazine* and went after it. She didn't need any mosquitoes in her room. Malaria she could do without. Had she taken her pills yesterday? She stood still for a moment, trying to remember. Yes, she had. Of course she had. It was the one thing she was absolutely meticulous about: taking her anti-malaria medicine every week.

She killed the mosquito with an ungodly whack of the magazine, the sound of it reverberating through the room, then she lay down on the bed and closed her eyes. She felt hot and sticky and wished she had an air-conditioner in her room. The humidity was practically dripping off the walls and everything felt damp, even the sheets. She had visions of herself waking up in the morning covered with mould. She thought of Mark, seeing in her mind his tall lean body stretched out on a comfortable bed in a cool room.

They said money couldn't buy you happiness, but it could certainly buy you comfort. And with a little more comfort she'd certainly be happy.

Happiness. She'd given up on true happiness a long time ago. She did very well without it. She had an interesting life, could do as she pleased, go where she pleased. She enjoyed her life in her own way and she'd learned to live with loneliness a long, long time ago.

The sun streaked hotly through the curtains when she awoke. There was a bathroom down the hall which was none too clean and she used it carefully, showering quickly in the thin stream of water, trying to touch as little as possible. Situations like this would have given her the shudders at home, but it was amazing what you could get used to. Having dressed in a blue cotton dress and flat leather sandals, she crossed the now empty lobby and went to the restaurant to have breakfast.

Mark was sitting in the middle of the room, and she saw him as soon as she entered. He was hard to miss, being tall and blond and the only white person in the place.

'Surprise, surprise,' she said, as she reached his table.

He grinned. 'Good morning, Sanny Joy.'

'Good morning. And please, drop the Joy. Sanny is bad enough all by itself.' She smiled cheerfully.

'Where did they get Sanny, anyway?' he asked. 'I've never heard of it.'

'It's from the San of San Francisco. My parents had a wild and wonderful affair there and it seems to be where I got my start, so to speak. Romantic, isn't it?' She smiled brightly.

'Very.' The tone of his voice gave nothing away.

Romantic like hell, she thought.

Her mother had been six months pregnant when her father finally married her. Sanny was three months old when he decided he'd made a mistake, so he had taken off and never come back. By the time Sanny was four years old her mother was a full-fledged alcoholic, and Sanny was taken away by the authorities and grew up in foster-homes. Too many foster-homes.

'So that's where Sanny Joy came from. Do you think the waiters have gone on strike?' Subject changed.

'There's one now,' he said, and sure enough one materialised at their table. Sanny ordered coffee and toast, and Mark looked at her disapprovingly.

'This one's on me, so order something decent. Have an omelette, a couple of eggs, whatever.'

'You're a prince, but no, thanks. I never have much for breakfast. And besides, Mr Professor, I am not poor and I am not starving.'

He gave her an expressionless glance, then turned to the waiter and ordered an omelette, toast and coffee.

'Why are you here, anyway?' Sanny asked, playing with a spoon. 'Wouldn't the girls let you leave last night?'

'Girls? Oh,' he grinned, 'to tell you the truth I had a couple of fascinating offers before I got out of there, but I scared them off.'

'Oh, how?'

'You wouldn't want to know.' His smile was charming, and she couldn't help laughing.

'You sound dangerous to me,' she observed.

'I'm a pussycat,' he said, his smile widening.

Hah! she thought. You don't fool me, Mr Professor. But she nodded in agreement. 'You look like one.'

He laughed. 'Here's the coffee.' It was placed in

front of them. 'Sugar, milk? Oh, that's right, I remember—black.' He drank from his coffee. 'Not bad. Tell me, what are you doing today?'

'I have no set plans. I do have to take back my rented typewriter and get my things in order. I'm leaving tomorrow.'

'Where are you going?' he asked.

'Up north—Yekepa. I have a college friend there. She married a Swedish engineer who works for the mining company up there.'

They talked about Sanny's travel plans all through breakfast. After they had finished eating Mark went with her to return the typewriter and they wandered around town together. He knew a lot about Liberia and its history, how American slaves had come back and settled the country, how some of the architecture resembled that of the southern United States. Until the government overthrow of a couple of years ago, the country had been ruled by descendants of the returned slaves, many of them bearing English names. It had been strange to discover, when she had first arrived, that Liberia used American currency.

Mark was lecturing at the University that afternoon and Sanny decided she wanted to hear what he had to say. Economics was not her forte, but Mark intrigued her and she wanted to know what it was exactly he was doing. The auditorium was large and packed to capacity with Liberian students. It was silent like a cave for more than an hour as Mark spoke. He sure could hold an audience, she thought with admiration. For almost another hour he answered questions.

'Wow,' she said afterwards, 'you were really good!'

'Thank you,' he replied gravely, eyes laughing.

'I even learned a few things.'

'That's a relief!'

A taxi took them back to his hotel where he took her to the bar for a drink. He invited her to stay for dinner, which she refused. She was starting to feel like a charity case, and she didn't need that. She'd been a charity case most of her life and she wasn't ever going to be in that position again.

'I have to pack, wash my hair, do some more work,' she offered as a reason. 'I'll have a quick bite at my hotel.'

'I'll join you there, then.' His eyes held hers and she began to feel warm.

'Why?'

'Why do you think?'

She feigned a thoughtful expression. 'You've fallen head over heels in love with me?'

'You guessed it.'

'Wow, I'm flattered—you a professor and me a stray!'

'I mean it,' he said, flashing white teeth in a charming smile.

She smiled back. 'So do I. And may I have another drink, please?'

She was served with another gin and tonic. She lifted her glass. 'Cheers. May your heart heal soon after I leave.'

'You have no tact,' said Mark, grinning. 'You're mocking my feelings.'

'Definitely not! I only hope you don't suffer too much. I wouldn't want anybody to suffer on my account—I'm not worth it.'

'Who says?'

'I say.' Sanny took a drink from her glass. 'Believe me, I know. I've broken a few hearts over the years. I don't know why that keeps happening.'

Of course she knew why it kept happening. Love 'em and leave 'em was the only way she could live and survive emotionally. All her life people had left her— her own mother, foster-parents, her first boy-friend in high school. It was not going to happen again. Nobody was going to leave her ever again. From now on she'd do the leaving. She was twenty-four now and she was doing just fine. It was easy enough to make friends. She got along with people very well, as long as all her relationships were on her own terms. Life was relatively easy without deep involvements. She wanted no complications—no more pain, no more sadness, no more unhappiness. The time for tears was past. Laughing was a lot healthier. So she laughed a lot, joked a lot, and made many friends. People liked her. She was doing well. There was an advantage in learning the lessons of life early on.

'Don't you worry about my heart,' said Mark. 'I'm a big boy.'

She nodded. 'Real big. Six foot two? Three?'

'Three. And you're a very little girl. Five foot what?'

'One. Lack of love,' she said casually. 'It'll stunt your growth. I read that in a magazine.'

'I have lots of love to give you,' he mocked.

'Thanks, but I think it's too late now.'

'You have a point there.' He looked at the glass in her hand. 'If you're done I'll take you back to your hotel so you can wash your hair and pack and do some more work and be ready by eight to have dinner with me.'

'You don't give up, do you?' she smiled ruefully.

'That's how I got to be a professor. I didn't give up.'

Sanny sighed as she slid off the bar stool. 'Well, I can't fight that.'

'Good. You're learning.' He grinned triumphantly.

Don't you get too cocky now, she said to him in silence. I can handle guys like you.

But could she really? Mark wasn't like any of the other men she'd known. For one thing, he was older and obviously more experienced in handling women.

He was amused by her, which was all right. A lot of men found her amusing. Only with him she had the uncomfortable feeling that he looked right through her. Behind the laughter in his eyes a multitude of thoughts were milling around—secret thoughts.

You're imagining things, she said to herself as she stood in the shower washing her hair. It was a good thing she had short hair or she'd never get the shampoo out of it under this miserly trickle of water. Tomorrow night she'd be at Laurie's house up north and surely there'd be a decent shower there. . . . She closed her eyes and pretended to feel the sheets of water streaming over her body. Ah, a shower like Niagara Falls! It would be heavenly.

Later she stared at her meagre supply of clothes wondering what to put on for dinner. It would have to be the long cotton dress again. It had been freshly washed and ironed by an employee of the hotel, but Sanny wished she had something else. Her other dresses were practical travel dresses and they were already showing signs of wear. Handwashing and drying in the sun had had their impact. Well, it didn't matter what she looked like, did it? Mark couldn't expect her to look like some glamour girl under the circumstances. She was on the road all the time and out in the bush often. That's where the stories were.

Her book was going to be good, she was very optimistic about that. It was going to be different from all the other books of its kind. She had decided on her own format and she was sure it would work.

It had better work, she thought dryly, or you'll end up in the poor house. Or you'll have to go back to work for the *Chronicle* and report on the openings of shopping centres and annual church rummage sales.

The thought alone was demoralising, and she groaned as she slid the dress over her head. There was no mirror in the room, so she rummaged through her bag to find the hand mirror and propped it up on the table, so she could apply some make-up. She didn't need much, just a little mascara and some lipstick. She had the best tan she'd ever had in her life and she liked the looks of it. With her dark brown eyes and her almost-black hair she looked positively Mediterranean with that dark skin.

Her hair was thick and curly and still quite damp. It would take a while to dry in the humidity. Lack of space had prevented her from bringing her blow-dryer. There were limits to what you could drag along with you if ease of movement was the greatest concern.

At eight o'clock sharp there was a rap on her door, and she went to open it. Mark. Dressed in light slacks and a dark shirt jacket open at the neck, he looked magnificent, and her heart gave a curious little leap.

'Come in. I thought we'd meet in the restaurant.'

'I didn't trust you.' He grinned down at her.

'That's quite a thing to say to a lady!' Sanny protested indignantly. 'Look at me, do I look as if. . . .'

'You look gorgeous.' He stepped forward, pulled her to him and kissed her.

It took a moment to register what was happening, then warmth flooded her and her heart began to pound. Her mind went blank. He kissed her very thoroughly, taking his time, and she stood in his arms as if hypnotised. When he let her go not a thought had entered her head and she stared at him, lost for words.

It was terrifying.

She wanted to say something. How could she not come up with something to say? There was a devilish gleam in his eyes.

'What's the matter?' he asked. 'Don't you know how to kiss?'

She swallowed and plastered on a smile. 'I'm out of practice.' Wrong, wrong.

'We can do something about that,' he said softly.

'Not now,' she said lightly. 'I'm starving. Didn't you say you wanted to join me for dinner?' She could still smell his clean soapy smell and the fragrance of his aftershave. She stepped back a little, opened the door and pointed to the hallway. 'This way, Professor.'

Her heart had stopped racing and her mind was working again. But there was no use denying that something had happened to her, and she wasn't sure if it excited her or terrified her. Maybe both.

'After you,' said Mark, lightly mocking. He grasped the door and she slid under his arm into the hall. Don't you laugh at me, Professor, she said silently. Next time you may not bowl me over quite so easily.

Next time? She was leaving tomorrow. Goodbye, Professor.

The meal served in the dining room of her hotel was mediocre, which was to be expected. Against her will and against her protestations Mark had ordered a bottle of wine, which he poured generously. Once it was in her glass how could she refuse? So she drank and he poured and she knew she was talking too much. The food didn't deserve much attention, so she swallowed it down with more wine. He was sipping while she was gulping and she realised it too late.

So, she thought, who cares? I feel fine. I enjoy a little wine now and then, a little conversation with a charming, intelligent man, who even pays for the whole thing to boot.

The thought almost sobered her right up. He wasn't going to pay for this meal! She informed him of the fact, and he gave her an exasperated look as if she were some dense, dimwitted student who didn't grasp a point after repeated explanations.

'I don't see why you have to make such an issue out of this,' he said reasonably. 'What's the harm in my paying for a meal?'

'It isn't just this meal,' she said stubbornly. 'You've been feeding me for the past twenty-four hours, and now it's my turn.'

'I wasn't counting turns,' he said. 'Hang on to your money. I have an uneasy feeling you're going to need it.'

She glowered at him. 'You're a male chauvinist. . . .' She swallowed 'pig' just in time. He was just trying to be nice. How did it happen that when men tried to be nice to women somehow it reduced them to the status of little girls who needed to be taken care of and pampered? She let out a theatrical sigh and finished the last of her wine.

'I didn't come here to be deluged by insults,' he said to her, glowering right back. 'I think we should have some coffee.'

Sanny gave up on the subject. She wasn't really in the mood for a full-fledged argument; she felt too pleasant for that. She started chattering about something else while they waited for the coffee to be served.

Later, after abandoning the vile-tasting coffee, Mark marched her through the lobby and up two flights of stairs back to her small room. He took the key from her nerveless fingers, opened the door and followed her in before she could do a thing about it.

Who did he think he was? Did he think he could fill her up with wine, waltz her into her room and. . . . Well, he had been right, hadn't he? He had done exactly that. But from now on she was in charge.

Why was she feeling so nervous? It was ridiculous! She looked at him leaning against the door, observing her with a lazy smile.

'I didn't invite you in,' she said charmingly.

'I know. You're not scared, are you?'

'Me? Scared? Of course not. You're a pussycat.'

He grinned. 'Sometimes a tiger.'

'I don't allow tigers in my room,' she told him.

'No? Why not?'

'They come on too strong.'

'I see.' He was smiling faintly as if hiding something. 'I'm sorry.'

'I'll bet,' she said sweetly. She looked directly at him, feeling a growing frustration. How was she going to get him out of the room? Was he just playing a little game, or was he really after her? Why wasn't he saying anything? Well, she wasn't going to stand there in silence.

'Since you are here,' she said, 'how about a drink? I have some warm bottled water and a can of milk powder if you care for a glass of milk.'

'I think I'll go home,' Mark said dryly, but he made no move. Hands in his pockets, he still stood leaning against the door, his posture one of lazy grace. She could easily picture him with a tennis racquet in his hand, tanned body clad in white—devastating.

She took a step forward. 'Thank you for a very nice time. I enjoyed your lecture. I hope you have a good time for the rest of your stay, and. . . .'

He laughed out loud, straightening away from the door. 'I really believe I had you worried there for a moment!'

She wasn't going to let him put her on the defensive again. Attack was the only strategy. She wasn't scared any more. Without thinking she moved towards him, stood on tiptoe and kissed him full on the mouth. Her heart was galloping wildly, her blood thundering in her head.

She pulled back. 'Goodbye, tiger.'

His hands came down on her shoulders and he gave her a look of amazed amusement.

'Oh no,' he said softly, 'it's not that easy.'

CHAPTER TWO

SHE'D made a monumental miscalculation. Frantically she reached behind her, grabbed the doorhandle and yanked the door open.

'You've got to go,' she said, smiling sunnily, 'or I'll scream the place down.'

'No, you won't.' Mark bent down, closed his mouth firmly over hers and proceeded to kiss her with slow, seductive deliberateness. Sanny felt herself melt right in his arms, the heady mixture of wine and sensual pleasure making her weak and spineless like a rag doll.

When he let her go she was lost and gone. She stared at him in a daze, seeing his smug little grin, the gleam in his eyes. Before she could collect herself, he strode through the open door, turned in the hall and beamed her a last smile.

'So long, Sanny Joy.'

He was gone. She slammed the door shut and sank down on the bed. 'So long, my foot, Professor,' she muttered nastily. 'Tomorrow I'm off and going and no way are you going to find me. West Africa is a very big place.'

A wave of unaccountable disappointment washed over her. It had been a terrific day. Last night had been equally terrific. Mark Taylor really was a terrific man.

No, he wasn't.

Why wasn't he here with her now? He hadn't gone when she told him to leave, and she'd thought he intended to stay after kissing her into submission. But no, he had marched right out, leaving her like *this*. Thinking about his kiss made her go warm all over.

He had no right. She closed her eyes, seeing in her mind's eye the tall, lean body, the blue, laughing eyes, the shiny blond hair.

She hoped that at his next lecture the students would boo him. She hoped somebody would offer him snail soup when he couldn't refuse. She hoped some ju-ju priest would cast a spell on him. She hoped. . . .

She threw herself forward into the pillow and burst into tears. Having calmed down she decided that what she needed was a glass of milk—cold milk. In the bathroom she washed her face, then ventured down through the lobby to the bar, staring with icy disdain at anybody who had the gall to lay eyes on her. From the bar she got a glass of water with ice in it. The water in town was safe to drink. Upstairs in her room she mixed milk powder into the water, stirred and waited until the mixture was good and cold, then fished out the remaining ice and dropped it in a water-glass.

Making herself comfortable on the bed with a pillow behind her back and her knees drawn up to her chin, she slowly drank the milk. It made her feel better—much better. Milk always did.

Next morning she gathered her things together and after breakfast lugged them outside and found a taxi to take her out of town to the coastal road. She shared the taxi with two women who chattered excitedly in one of the many local languages. One of them had a newborn baby who was sound asleep in its mother's lap wrapped in a yellow knit blanket that would have been warm enough in sub-zero weather.

Sanny hitched her way down the coast, catching one ride to Marshall in a decrepit V.W. with a skinny young man who boasted that he was the owner of a rubber plantation. His story was rather leaky and she didn't believe a word of it, but he was amusing company and she was grateful for the ride. From Marshall to Buchanan she rode with a German missionary who told her that soul-saving was out of fashion and that for Christians there was a lot to be learned from the so-called primitive religions of the world. He seemed to be having a wonderful time, which was, as far as Sanny was concerned, the only way to live your life if you had any choice.

If you had any choice. Sometimes, of course, fate was not on your side, but even when circumstances were negative, positive sides could be found. If life gives you lemons, make lemonade. She'd become quite adept at finding sugar to sweeten her life.

She found herself some lunch and bought some peanuts and bananas to ward off starvation while she spent the entire afternoon on the railbus crossing the country from Buchanan to Yekepa.

It was a long afternoon, with the scenery almost unchanging bushy jungle. Here and there were some clearings with thatched-roof mud huts and some cultivated plots of land. Sanny distinguished corn, cassava and some rice, and felt pleased about her growing knowledge. There were no towns and she hoped fervently the rail-bus would keep going and not have some unfortunate malfunction. Breaking down in the middle of this jungle was an adventure she could do without, even though it might result in an exciting story.

Laurie was waiting for her on the small platform when they arrived in Yekepa. Tall, blonde and gorgeous, she looked cool and clean in a pale blue dress, making Sanny feel instantly grubby and dirty in the well-worn and washed dress that had lost much of its colour in the sunshine.

It was *so* good to see her, said Laurie with somewhat uncharacteristic enthusiasm. Sanny felt herself embraced and hugged with more uncharacteristic enthusiasm. Laurie had never been one to show a lot of outward affection, had always adopted a pose of calm self-possessing, had an unruffled demeanour that Sanny sometimes envied.

A young boy in a tattered shirt helped carry the luggage to Laurie's shiny white Peugeot. During the short ride to Laurie's house, Sanny sat, stunned, through an emotional outpouring of Laurie's miseries. She hated this stupid little town. She hated the people in it. She hated her husband who was fooling around with a German nurse. She hated her life. She hated herself.

Well, Sanny thought dryly, I guess I don't need to ask how she is.

'You know what he says?' Laurie said viciously, talking of her husband. 'He says I'm a spoiled, egotistical nag. He says I should have stayed home and married a dentist!'

There was wisdom in those words, Sanny decided, feeling rather disloyal in thinking it. She'd never understood why Laurie had married Bengt. For one thing, she hadn't known him very long. For another thing, her ideas of a good life included a house in one of Boston's classy neighbourhoods, a yacht, and vacations in the Caribbean. Marrying a Swedish engineer who worked in Africa wouldn't do the job, although it had to be said that Bengt certainly had things to offer. He was tall and handsome and sexy. He was intelligent and made good money. He was probably good in bed, which was likely to be the reason Laurie had married him, Sanny thought cynically.

After Sanny had been shown to her room, which was as attractive and comfortable as the rest of the low white bungalow, she stripped and stood in the shower for a long time, feeling the cool water pour over her in generous invigorating streams. Ah, how lovely! She sighed from pure delight.

Having dressed in her long cotton dress, she went in search of Laurie. She found her in the kitchen giving instructions to the cook.

'Let's have some wine and sit outside. It's cooling down,' Laurie suggested, taking a bottle of white wine out of the refrigerator. 'Here, take these glasses.' She handed them to Sanny and picked up a board with cheese and crackers and led the way out.

'Bengt is working late,' she said sarcastically, 'and he offers his apologies to you. He'll see you later.'

Not much of Laurie's cool, calm demeanour was left, and Sanny observed her friend with growing amazement.

'I'm not going to be of much help, you know,' she said. 'I'm not an expert on marriage and I haven't any idea of what the problem is.'

'You know about men,' Laurie said, pouring wine into the glasses.

Sanny shrugged. 'Some. Enough to know that marriage isn't for me.'

'I should have listened to you,' Laurie said bitterly. 'You told me not to marry the jerk.'

Bengt is not a jerk, Sanny thought, remembering. 'Personally, I'd rather be free than anything,' she said. 'It's easiest, anyway. You get involved with another person on an emotional level and everything becomes too complicated. I don't need it.' She bent over and cut off a piece of Edam cheese. 'This is great. It's weeks since I had a decent piece of cheese. Where do you get it?'

'At the store,' Laurie said dryly. 'Imported, of course.'

The wine was cool and dry and very refreshing. Dark had come quickly, bringing with it cooler night air. Away from the coast and at a higher altitude the climate was definitely more comfortable, less humid and cooler at night. The porch with its potted plants and comfortable chairs was a perfect place to sit and relax after a hot day.

'It's lovely here,' said Sanny. 'I like your house.'

'Wait till you live here for a year!' sighed Laurie.

'What is so bad about living here?'

'I like Boston.'

We knew that, Sanny thought, forcing down a sigh of exasperation. 'This seems to be a perfectly nice little town,' she said reasonably. 'You told me there's a big swimming pool, a tennis club, a golf course, a library, and you told me there are a lot of other expatriates around here, working for the mine, so what else do you want?'

Laurie's expression spoke volumes. She wanted Boston. So then why had she come out here? Maybe Bengt was right. Maybe Laurie was spoiled. She should have married a dentist. Sanny noticed Laurie was working on her second glass of wine. It made her think of last night, when she herself had been drinking wine, glass after glass. She thought of Mark.

She began to feel warm all over. She could feel his kiss again, his arms around her. It was the most ridiculous thing that had ever happened to her. She'd known him for twenty-four hours and the thought of him alone evoked all kinds of mixed emotions in her.

With an effort she dragged her attention back to Laurie, who was staring morosely into her glass, slender legs elegantly crossed at the ankles. 'Why did you marry him when you knew you'd have to live out here?' she queried.

'Because I was in love with him,' Laurie said with bitter anger. 'He bowled me over with his sexy accent and that indecent tan in the middle of January. He was so damn charming and so damn sophisticated.' She shrugged. 'I was deaf, dumb and blind. I was ready to follow him to the ends of the earth, which is exactly what I ended up doing.'

No, you didn't, Sanny said silently. As long as you can sit here drinking wine and eating cheese and as long as you can go to a library and swim in a swimming pool you are not at the end of the world. Laurie, my girl, you haven't seen a thing yet.

She wouldn't have the slightest desire to see it either, Sanny realised. If Laurie knew about the way she had been living these past two months, she'd have a fit. She wondered how they had managed to be such good friends during college. It certainly seemed that they didn't have much in common any more. People change with the circumstances—it was an easy answer, maybe even true.

'How did you change so fast?' Sanny asked. 'If you were so crazy about him, none of this should have mattered a bit.' She shrugged. 'At least that's what they say. I can't say I know about it from experience.' And may I never know about it from experience, she prayed silently. Love, if that was what it was, caused a lot of misery for a lot of people. She, Sanny Joy, was going to avoid misery like the plague.

'I don't know—oh, I guess I do.' Laurie sighed. 'We came here, and suddenly everything changed. Bengt had to go to work every day and I sat at home here twiddling my thumbs. Suddenly I wasn't the only important thing in his life any more. He takes his job so damned seriously, he's practically married to it. You know why he married me? He was tired of the bachelor's life. He'd decided that before he came back here again he'd have a wife to join him. I doubt he ever really loved me.' She gulped down the rest of her wine and reached for the bottle again. 'Anyway, now he's got himself this adoring little German nurse, and I'm about as superfluous as a fifth wheel on a wagon.'

'What are you going to do?' asked Sanny.

'I'm going to leave, what else? I'm not going to sit

here and suffer for the hell of it. I was going to ask. . . .'

Oh, help! Sanny thought.

Laurie hesitated. 'I was wondering, when you go back south, if I couldn't come with you.'

'I'm not going back south,' Sanny told her. 'I was planning to go east to the Ivory Coast. There must be a way to get there from here without having to go back to the coast.'

'I wouldn't know.' Laurie looked at Sanny with a puzzled expression. 'What have you been doing, just travelling around? I can't imagine it being a lot of fun, all by yourself.'

'I'm working.' She explained what she was doing.

'What about your job at the *Chronicle*?'

Sanny shrugged. 'I quit. I wanted to do this—travel, meet people, see something of the world.'

'What if I came with you?'

She couldn't believe her ears. 'Laurie, you're crazy! You wouldn't like it! I stay in cheap hotels. I hitch-hike, or go on local buses. I eat by the road. You wouldn't last a day.' Not sleek, slender, comfort-loving Laurie.

Laurie looked down in her glass. 'No, I suppose you're right.'

'Why don't you take the rail-bus to Buchanan, take a bus back to Robert's Field and get yourself on a plane?'

'That's what I'll have to do. Let's eat.' Laurie got up, smiling brightly. 'The hell with it all! Absalom's cooked us a beautiful meal, let's enjoy it. And while we're eating, tell me about your adventures.'

It was with great relief that Sanny left Yekepa a few days later. Staying with Laurie was depressing and there was not a thing she could do for her. Some friend she was, she thought, feeling almost guilty, but not quite. She couldn't help but feel impatient and exasperated with Laurie's problems. Laurie had been stupid. She should have stayed in Boston and married a dentist. From all the stories Laurie had told her over the last few days it was quite obvious that the failure of her marriage was at least as much her fault as it was Bengt's, who could have had the decency not to start an affair in front of the whole town. That kind of behaviour was unforgivable.

Sanny breathed a sigh of relief as she climbed into the cabin of a gravel truck on its way to the border post.

A week later she arrived in Abidjan with an entire notebook full of stories, notes, anecdotes and interviews to be typed up. She found a small hotel not far from the centre of town, went out and rented a typewriter, struggling with her French once more, and went back to her hotel to spend the next few days working. She went out only once, to the American Consular Office to check if anyone had tried to contact her from home, and to report her presence in the country.

The food in the hotel was French and quite good, and having eaten a rather monotonous diet for the last week, Sanny was delighted with the change. She was anxious to start exploring the city, but forced herself to finish her work first. She wrote three columns for the travel section of the *Chronicle* and mailed them separately. The next day she sent off a copy of each of them, separately again, to ensure that something would arrive. The mail was not exactly reliable.

She was ready to go down for dinner when a knock came on the door. She opened it, expecting the delivery of her clean clothes, but instead found herself staring at a broad chest clad in a green shirt jacket. As she looked up, her gaze met the bright blue of Mark Taylor's eyes.

'*Bonsoir,*' *mademoiselle.*' He stepped past her into the room.

'*Bonsoir* yourself,' she answered lightly, terrified he would hear the thundering of her heart. What's the *matter* with me? she thought in a panic. Her legs were shaking and she could barely think. Breathing seemed suddenly difficult. This man was dangerous to her health.

He looked terrific. She stared at him silently and he began to laugh. 'How are you? Did you have a nice visit with your friend in Yekepa?'

'Delightful,' she said. 'And how are you?'

'Extremely well, especially these last two minutes.'

'And your lectures?'

'A great success everywhere.'

Apparently the students had not booed him. He didn't look as if some ju-ju priest had cast some evil spell on him, either.

'Did you enjoy your snail soup?' she asked.

'My *what*?'

'Snail soup,' she said stony-faced. 'Nobody offered you snail soup? I didn't think so.'

'What's this all about?' he demanded.

She smiled sunnily. 'Nothing. Forget it. I'm on my way down to dinner. Would you like to join me?'

He gave her a hard stare. 'You are weird,' he declared.

'I'm glad you noticed. Are you coming?' She picked up her bag, swung it over her shoulder and flounced out the door. Mark followed her, closing the door behind him.

'Don't you want this locked?' he asked calmly.

'Oh, yes, of course. My key ... is in here somewhere.' Hastily Sanny scrabbled through the contents of her bag. Where are you, stupid key? It took a while to locate it. He made her nervous standing there waiting for her, cool, calm and collected. At last she felt the cold metal against her hand and jerked it out of the bag and locked the door. Her hand was shaking.

'Let's find a decent place to eat,' he said, steering her right out of the hotel before she had a chance to protest.

'The food is fine!' she said angrily, standing stock still on the pavement in front of the hotel. 'I've eaten here for four days straight and I haven't died yet!'

'You're lucky. It's time for a change, I'd say. I will treat you to the best Abidjan has to offer.'

'You're such a snob! What's wrong with plain food?'

'Nothing at all. Don't be difficult, Sanny Joy.'

'Don't call me Sanny Joy!'

'Sorry, I forgot.' He waved at a taxi. It moved over to the kerb and Mark manoeuvred her into it without further argument.

How can I let this happen? Sanny thought wildly. Nobody has ever treated me this way. Nobody has ever made me do this to myself. I'm nothing but a child being manipulated. I can't let this happen!

In mute silence she sat next to him and he made no comment for the short ride to the restaurant.

'Now,' he said as they were seated, 'if you're over your tantrum we can enjoy the evening.'

'I don't like the way you treat me,' she complained.

'Oh? How do I treat you?'

'You don't take me seriously.'

There was a gleam in his eyes. 'I take you very seriously, Sanny.'

'Not the way I mean! You ignore my wishes. You discount my reasons for wanting something. It's not very respectful, you know! I don't like to feel manipulated.'

He groaned. 'Good God, I didn't know it was that bad! I must be a terrible person.'

'See? You don't even take this seriously! You just make fun of me!'

'I just don't like to make big issues out of little things. All I want is a nice meal in a nice restaurant with a nice woman. I was looking forward to this evening. I'm glad I found you again.'

How could she be angry when he smiled so charmingly? How could she be angry when he looked at her with those laughing blue eyes? She would save her anger for another time. Mark hadn't won the argument, only postponed it. She didn't feel like pushing her points just now. She sighed, the uneasy thought stirring that no matter how right she was, she might never win an argument with him. But it would certainly be worth a try, one day, when she was in really fine shape. She was looking forward to it already.

One day when? Good heavens she was talking as if he was a fixture in her life. He might be flying off to Timbuctoo tomorrow for all she knew.

He took her hand. 'I *am* glad I found you again, you know.'

'You flatter me,' she said, smiling ravishingly. 'How *did* you find me? How did you know I was in Abidjan?'

'You told me, remember?'

'I did? Oh, I guess I did. How did you find me here? Did you check out every second-rate hotel in town?'

He grinned. 'I had somebody do it for me. How about a drink before dinner?'

It was crazy, something out of a book. It gave her the weirdest feeling, not unpleasant exactly, just ... she was at a loss for the right word. She eyed him suspiciously.

'You're not serious, are you?' she asked.

'About the drink? Oh, absolutely.'

She let out an exasperated sigh. 'About having hired

somebody to find me in this town.'

He nodded gravely. 'Very serious. Sanny. I told you I'd see you again. You aren't surprised, are you?' His eyes lightly mocked her.

'*Of course* I'm surprised. Also, I'm not sure I like the idea of somebody trying to trail me, somebody snooping around asking about me.'

'He was just a kid. This town is full of very enterprising young men who'd gladly do a day's work if they could find a job. Besides, this isn't New York City. There's a limit to the number of second-rate hotels to look in, and it only took him a few hours. Now how about that drink?'

Sanny ordered some wine and decided to forget it. If the Professor wanted to spend his money on tracing her down, what did she care? Well, she did care. She'd inspect her feelings about it later, in the quiet safety of her room.

'Are you in town to work?' she asked.

He nodded. 'Of course. I have to keep to my schedule. I arrived here this morning, and I'll be here for the next several days.'

'And then?'

'I'll be off to Nigeria.'

Good, she thought, out of the way. She drank her wine.

'And you're going on to Ghana, right?' he added.

'Yes, I guess I told you that, too.'

'You did.'

The waiter appeared at their table to take their orders and Sanny's eyes ran along the menu quickly, hungrily. There were a variety of steaks, and quite a few seafood dishes, including shrimp and lobster. Shrimp in white wine sauce. Lobster Thermidor. Lobster in cheese sauce. Decisions, decisions.

'I'll have the lobster in cheese sauce.' It was probably one of the most expensive dishes, but she couldn't tell because, in good old-fashioned male chauvinist tradition, the lady's menu did not display the prices.

'An appetiser?' asked Mark.

'Avocado with vinaigrette dressing, please.' She was going to enjoy this meal. She might as well.

Mark ordered a shrimp cocktail and Lobster Thermidor for the main course and asked to see the wine list, which the waiter had conveniently ready.

In true-blue European style, the food was slow in coming. They spent the time in leisurely conversation, sipping wine. Sanny told Mark all about her trip through the country, of having spent two days at a lumber camp where exquisite tropical hardwood trees were cut and prepared for transport to the southern ports from where the timber would be shipped all over the world. She talked about the cocoa and coffee plantations she had visited, and the people she had met, who had all been most co-operative, friendly and hospitable. Mark seemed to find it interesting and he listened intently, asking questions now and then.

It was late when dinner was over. She felt happy and satiated and warm with wine and good cheer. They went back to her hotel in a relic of a taxi. The stuffing was coming out of the cushions and the glass in one of the side windows was gone. The driver wore a T-shirt with the slogan '*Vive la différence*' on his chest and a blue knitted ski hat on his head. In the restaurant you could easily pretend not to be in Africa, but in this taxi it was quite impossible.

'Thank you very much for a wonderful evening,' she said graciously, standing in front of her hotel room door.

'You're quite welcome. Aren't you going to invite me in?' Mark's eyes were laughing and slightly mocking.

'I wouldn't want to give you the wrong impression,'

she said sweetly. 'Besides, I have no drinks to offer except. . . .'

'Instant milk—I know. I know. I'll go down to the bar and have them send something up. I want to talk to you. I have a suggestion.'

A suggestion or a proposition? She didn't want him in her room. She was no fool. She'd never get him out. He could forget it.

'It's late—I'm tired,' she sighed.

Mark took her left hand and looked at her wrist watch. 'It's only a quarter to eight.'

'My watch has retired. It's been a quarter to eight for a long time.'

'At least for the last two weeks. I noticed it in Monrovia. Why do you wear a broken Mickey Mouse watch?'

'Because it's better than not wearing a broken Mickey Mouse watch,' she said evenly.

'Of course,' he said, nodding in agreement, 'that's reasonable.' He didn't let go of her hand, instead pulled her to him. 'Open the door,' he whispered in her ear.

'I have a headache,' she whispered back, her heart throbbing wildly. She smelled the familiar clean soapy smell, the same light fragrance of aftershave. Her cheek was almost touching his chest and it took an effort to keep from resting against him. It would feel very comfortable.

'I'm not going to ravish you against your will,' he whispered.

No. He'd probably do it with her full co-operation. Oh, God, this was ridiculous. Why was she so nervous? Why was she acting like a teenager out on her first date?

'Give me the damned key,' Mark said softly, taking her right hand and uncurling her fingers one by one from around the key. Sanny offered no resistance. I'm doing it again, she thought in detached amazement. I let him walk all over me. Why do I let this happen?

He opened the door and gently pushed her inside, then closed it behind them. He put the key on the table without locking the door, then came towards her and rested his hands on her shoulders, looking straight into her eyes.

'I'm in love with you,' he said.

Her heart was going to give out, she was sure. Her blood was racing hotly through her.

'You said that before. I'm sorry.'

'Sorry? Why are you sorry?'

'It's obvious. I'm not the easiest person to be in love with. It's not very practical. I travel a lot.' She managed a bright smile. 'How about that drink? I've changed my mind. I think I'd like one.'

'Your enthusiasm for the subject is touching,' Mark said dryly. He looked at her with contemplation in his eyes, then slowly bent his head and kissed her. His mouth was firm and demanding. His hands slipped off her shoulders and down her back, drawing her closely to him. Her breasts were pressing against him and she closed her eyes, feeling a lightheadedness overtake her. Her arms moved around him and she responded to his kiss because she couldn't do anything else. She felt herself slipping, which was not what she intended to do. With other men she'd always been in perfect control over her emotions as well as her actions.

With the remnants of sanity, she broke free, looked up into his face and smiled sunnily. 'I'm going to die of asphyxiation if you don't cut that out, Professor. You wouldn't want to end up with a body, would you? I hear African jails are no garden spots. . . .' She pulled down the long, loose sleeves of her dress and raked her hands through her hair, trying with an effort to get her breathing and her heartbeat under control.

For a few silent moments Mark surveyed her with

amused interest. 'I can see you're going to be a challenge.'

'I sure hope so. Did you say something about a drink?'

'You have a real knack for changing the subject, don't you?'

'I get bored real easy,' she shrugged.

'Bored?' His eyes were dancing. 'Oh, so that's what it was. I see. Well, we'd better get you that drink. I won't be long.' In passing he picked up the key from the table. 'Just in case,' he said, grinning, and strode out of the door.

Just in case what? Just in case she'd lock him out, that's what. The Professor was no dummy. Well, neither am I, Sanny thought mutinously. I'll have to find a way to deal with him.

It was easy being brave and feeling secure when he wasn't in the room to throw her all off balance. She'd always been able to conduct her friendships and relationships with other men with a certain kind of detachment. It made it easy to break free. It made it easy not to get hurt. It made it easy to have a good time without worry. Treating everything lightly and taking nothing seriously was a very successful tactic, and it had always worked.

So why was it not working now? What was so different about Mark Taylor?

Sanny sighed dramatically. If I knew the answer to that one, she thought, I'd be able to find a way to handle him.

A moment later he strode back into the room, all six feet three of him, and she admitted to herself right then and there that he didn't look like a man anybody could handle. He did all the handling himself.

'They say they'll be here with the drinks in ten minutes, which probably means anything between thirty minutes and an hour,' he told her. 'What are your plans for tomorrow?'

He parked himself next to her on the bed. It was the only comfortable place to sit, she had to admit, but she wished he'd taken the straight chair that went with the table. She moved slightly away, meeting his mocking eyes with challenge.

'I haven't seen much of Abidjan yet. I was going to look around tomorrow. I've been working mostly, these last few days.'

Mark said he was busy in the afternoon, but free in the morning, and without realising it Sanny found herself agreeing to spending the morning hours with him. He had a terribly persistent manner about him which wasn't really very obvious until it was too late. Deceptive is what he is, she thought warily. He knows how to manipulate me. It was not an admission she relished making.

The drinks arrived and she found herself sipping some mysterious concoction that was sweet and delicious but undeniably potent. Careful, careful, she admonished herself, don't you let him get away with his evil intentions.

'It's stifling in here,' he commented, getting up from the bed and checking out the window. 'It won't open any further than this?'

'It's stuck, I think. I tried.' She shrugged. 'You can't have everything.'

'Next time we'll have our little meetings in my hotel room,' he decided. 'I don't need to suffer through this when there's a perfectly cool, air-conditioned place we can be.'

'You invited yourself, remember?'

He gave her a dark, sinister glare. 'Did I have a choice?'

'Of course. You could have gone to that delicious room of yours in that luscious hotel.'

'Alone, yes. Unless I wanted to drag you in there by

the hair.' He pushed and pulled at the window and swore under his breath. 'All right, hang on,' he warned. 'I'm going to give it a whack.'

Sanny nearly hit the ceiling. It was a whack all right, a god-awful whack, and the splintering sounds coming from the window frame made her fear the worst.

'It's open,' Mark said unnecessarily. 'It may never close again, but at least we have some air now.'

'Thanks a lot,' she said sarcastically. 'And tomorrow I'll find the place robbed.'

'Not on the third floor. It'd be extremely difficult to climb the outside walls, especially with all this traffic coming through the street. I considered it all, don't worry.'

He'd considered it all, had he? How very thoughtful. She sipped carefully from the drink, watching the athletic, virile body in front of her. She wished she didn't feel so hopelessly attracted to him. She wished she didn't keep asking herself what it would be like to make love with him. She wished she could keep her heart and nerves under better control. She wished he would kiss her again, because it was really a wonderful, magical feeling.

She sighed deeply, feeling quite lightheaded with the drink warming her blood and her thoughts quickening her pulse.

Mark sat down next to her again and she felt herself being enveloped in his embrace, and it was really quite wonderful. She lifted her mouth to his and began to kiss him, not caring that her emotions were carrying her away and that her mind was slipping again. . . .

He responded to her kisses with a surprising passion—or maybe it was not so surprising. His hands moved down her body, gently touching, caressing. Sanny didn't fight the emotions flooding her—she couldn't. It was all too intoxicating, too. . . .

It was all feeling and sensation ... the touch of his lips on her eyes and temples, the warmth of his hands penetrating the thin cotton of her dress, the blood rushing through her, the irregular beating of her heart.

His hands moved up and took her face between them and he moved back a little to look at her.

'That was better,' he said softly. There was a smile in his eyes, but no mockery.

She felt warm and flushed and her breathing was uneven, and she wished he wouldn't see her like this, all shaky and trembling and out of control. She took his hands away from her face, bent her head and closed her eyes.

'Did you give me that drink so you could seduce me?' she muttered.

He laughed softly, drawing her close again. 'No. I just wanted to loosen you up enough so you'd let yourself feel something.'

'What's that supposed to mean?' Why did she ask? She knew exactly what he meant.

'I think you know. You were nervous and uptight— I'm not sure why.'

'You imagine things,' she murmured, rubbing her cheek against his shoulder. It felt so good sitting here like this in the circle of his arms, feeling sweet temptation rising in her, a longing for more than kisses and caresses. Not now, she thought vaguely. Not so easily. . . .

'Are you falling asleep?' he whispered.

Sanny made a small affirmative sound. 'That's what happens when I drink too much.' Oh, if only he knew!

'In that case, I'd better let you go to bed.' He sounded faintly amused. She'd thought he'd be disappointed. He released her and leaped to his feet with amazing energy. He stood towering over her, looking down on her, and she stared back at him, dazed.

'Are you leaving?' she asked.

'Do you want me to stay?'

Yes, more than anything else.

'No,' she said. 'I'm too tired.'

Mark nodded sympathetically. 'And a headache coming on, too, I can tell.'

'It's your own fault. You shouldn't have given me that drink double strength.' She smiled sweetly.

'I think you're misinterpreting my motives,' Mark said lightly, moving to the door.

I'll bet, she thought.

'Sleep tight, Sanny.' He grinned and opened the door. 'Sweet dreams. See you tomorrow.'

Tomorrow ... they were going to spend the morning together. A memory stirred. He'd said something about a suggestion but hadn't mentioned it again, and she had forgotten to ask in the confusion and excitement of what followed. Maybe it had been just a come-on, a way to get into her room. First thing in the morning she'd ask him. Sanny sighed and got ready for bed.

Dressed in a leafy-green dress and sandals, she was ready for him when he knocked on her door the next morning.

He looks better every day, she thought, feeling herself leap to life at the sight of him standing in the door—tall and athletic, wearing light summer slacks and a white shirt. She liked his face—an interesting face with strong, masculine features His blue eyes met hers and she smiled serenely, feeling a very unserene tug at her heart.

Don't tell me, she said to herself, you're in love. So? You've been in love before. You know how to handle that. Take it easy, take it slow, and for heaven's sake don't take it seriously.

No, she thought. Don't do that. Don't ever do that.

CHAPTER THREE

'READY?' asked Mark.

Sanny nodded, swung her bag over her shoulder and followed him out the door.

'Listen,' she said as they emerged into the hot, humid morning air, 'last night you said you had a suggestion, but you didn't say what.'

'I did? Oh, that's right. It's about your trip to Ghana.'

'What about my trip to Ghana?'

He hailed a taxi and they climbed in. In beautifully modulated French tones he told the driver where to take them. Sanny envied him. Her French was adequate, but she didn't sound half as polished and competent as Mark did.

He turned to face her. 'I have some very good friends in Accra, Matt and Jackie Simmons. They've lived in Africa for several years now and they'd be a good resource for you. They work for a non-profit-making development agency and do a fair bit of travelling around. They could give you some good leads for stories, and they know some interesting Ghanaians you might like to talk to. I'm sure they could be of help to you.'

Sanny felt a surge of excitement. Good contacts were invaluable, she'd found that out very soon after arriving. 'Sounds great,' she said with enthusiasm. 'You don't think they'd mind me hanging around and making a general nuisance of myself?'

'I wouldn't have suggested it, if I thought that,' he returned patiently. 'As a matter of fact, they'll probably ask you to stay with them. They have a nice little guest flat that's always ready for whomever needs a place to stay.'

'Oh, I couldn't! I can't expect perfect strangers to put me up. It's not necessary. It'll be great just to get a chance to talk to them.'

'You mention my name and you'll be a friend for life,' he said with a smug little grin. 'You'll like them. Do think about it. It's almost impossible to find a decent hotel at a reasonable price in Accra. The economic situation is not very encouraging at the moment and prices are sky high.'

'There are always indecent hotels,' she said lightly, remembering the Arrivederci in Monrovia. 'I can fend for myself. I've slept in some pretty terrible places. Don't worry about me.'

Mark gave her a dark look. 'Well, you'll see for yourself,' he said gloomily. 'I know you're intent on being heroic about your adventures, and I do admire you, but that's no reason to turn down a good meal and a clean bed when they're offered to you.'

Sanny laughed. 'When you talk like that, I almost feel sorry for myself.'

The morning went by quickly. There was much to see and much to do, and Mark's company made all the difference in the world. His comments gave an extra dimension to her observations and she valued his input. He'd been to Africa many times over the years and he knew so much . . . it was maddening. Her own ignorance bothered her. Having him with her was stimulating and exhilarating, and she felt very much alive. It had been a long time since she'd last felt so animated in a man's company. How long? She couldn't even remember. It had never been quite like this. She felt positively bubbly, like a tub full of soapsuds.

But tomorrow she had to leave.

No, I don't, she thought. I can stay for a few more

days. Mark isn't leaving for Nigeria until Tuesday.

You'd better play it safe, said her Other Self from somewhere inside her. You might get addicted to this man, and then you're in real trouble.

I can handle it, she thought bravely.

You'd better watch out.

Oh, shut up, she thought irritably, and the voice inside her retreated.

Mark had work to do that afternoon and she spent the rest of the day alone, doing some shopping in the open market, buying toothpaste and new batteries for her flashlight. Everything in the world was available in the small stalls—plastic dolls from Hong Kong, native and imported medicines, fresh and dried fish, matches and shoe-laces and sunglasses, charcoal and baskets and pots, bread and bras and beads—too much to mention. Everything was displayed in neat and orderly fashion, arranged anew every morning, packed up late every afternoon.

Tonight she'd have dinner with Mark again; she'd stopped fighting it, deciding she might as well enjoy it. Who knew what she'd be eating by the road tomorrow? Cassava with some fishy sauce, fried plantain, roasted maize, bread and fish. . . . She'd sit in a little chop bar or in the shade of some big avocado tree, surrounded by giggling children watching her with fascination. A white woman eating African-style was the weirdest thing they'd seen in months and they had no qualms about showing their interest. It had been difficult at first to eat in peace with half a village of children staring at her every movement, but she was used to it by now. Privacy did not seem to be a well understood concept, she had discovered.

That night she enjoyed the quiet surroundings of the fashionable restaurant where Mark had taken her, ate with relish the French food and drank with moderation of the French wine until she felt light and happy—but not too light and not too happy. She kissed him goodnight in front of her door, said he couldn't come in, wished him a good trip to Nigeria and thanked him for everything.

It was a courageous try but totally ineffectual. Taking the key from her unwilling hand, he opened the door and pushed her into the room ahead of him.

Sanny felt a flash of fear—not so much about what he might say or do, but more about what she herself might say or do. All during the day she'd been keenly aware of the currents and vibrations between them, of something happening. Her Other Self had been commenting all day on her thoughts and feelings, which was a bother, a nuisance, and an irritation, as well as a bad sign. Her Other Self was an important part of her make-up. It served as a well-developed warning device that had protected her from many follies in the past. It had been working at full capacity all day and she was beginning to feel a growing apprehension.

Mark planted himself squarely in front of the door, legs slightly apart, thumbs hooked behind his belt, eyes full of some dark determination.

'I'm getting mixed signals,' he stated calmly. 'How about some clarification?'

'I don't know what you mean.' Sanny made her voice toneless, her face expressionless.

'Don't play dumb.' There was an edge of irritation to his voice now. 'Why are you so eager to get rid of me suddenly?'

'I'm not into one-night stands,' she retorted coolly.

'Very commendable, but I don't remember making the suggestion.'

Anger flared. 'Well, I'm *not* exactly *dense*, you know! You comb the town to find me, you wine and dine me, you come on to me in no uncertain way— what *am* I supposed to expect?'

'You come on to me too,' Mark countered quietly.

'I am not!' She was lying out of sheer fright. She was hopelessly attracted to him and she was losing her cool, which was another bad sign. She wanted him out of her room before she did do something she'd regret later. He stood there, radiating virility and sex appeal, and she knew that if he'd make even half an attempt at seducing her she'd be a willing victim. She was beginning to feel jittery under his sceptical regard.

'Why are you denying it?' he asked. 'You know there's something between us, so why not go with the flow? Isn't that what's normally done?'

'And end up in bed?' she suggested caustically.

A casual shrug. 'If it's mutually agreeable, and when the time is right.'

'Well, it's not mutually agreeable,' she said, trying desperately to sound calm, 'and the time is not right and I don't want to.' She did not sound calm. She sounded like a frightened virgin, which was not the effect she was after.

She read the exasperation in his eyes, saw the hardening of his face.

'Then just say so, for God's sake. I'm not some raving rapist! But don't act as if you're more than happy with my company one minute and then want to shove me out of the way the next. I don't go for that kind of duplicity.'

'Why don't you just get out of here?' she suggested in her sweetest voice. 'I don't know why we have this conversation—I'm leaving tomorrow.'

There was a slight pause. 'I had intended to ask you to stay on for a few more days until I leave for Nigeria,' Mark said slowly, looking right at her.

Sanny had had the same idea herself. There was no reason why she couldn't stay.

Yes, there is, said her Other Self. Warning signals flashed frantically in her mind. Mark Taylor was dangerous to her health, to her peace of mind, to her long fought-for mental equilibrium. Mark Taylor, if she gave him half a chance, would have the power to make or break her. And a long time ago she'd vowed, cursing and weeping, that no one would ever, ever have that kind of power over her again.

She squared her shoulders and clenched her hands into fists. 'I couldn't say.'

'Why not?'

'I have my reasons.' She felt amazingly calm, suddenly. It was the right thing to do. Staying around here and spending more time with him could prove to be disastrous. 'I want you to leave now. Please.' She looked right at him, not wavering.

He came towards her and she backed away, but there was no place to go. He pulled her tense body into his arms and began to kiss her fiercely, possessively. She felt overpowered, physically as well as emotionally, felt her calm and determination flutter away like dry leaves in an autumn breeze.

When he released her, she was trembling. He looked at her for a long, silent moment and the air vibrated with nameless emotion. The knowledge was like a current between them: *You feel what I feel. There's something special between us.*

She swallowed hard. 'I'd appreciate it,' she said shakily, 'if you'd leave now.'

Without a word he turned and strode out of the room.

She should have known better than to think she'd never see him again. With a painful lurch of her heart she saw him sitting in the lobby of her hotel the next morning when she came down to check out. He looked quite comfortable, draped in a chair, his legs stretched out to their full length, as if prepared to wait all day. He was wearing an old pair of jeans and a sports shirt, and on his head perched a khaki bush hat. Next to him on the floor lay an army duffel bag that looked as if it dated back to the Civil War.

Sanny took in the scene in silent despair, her mouth suddenly dry.

'What are you doing here?' she asked at last.

Mark looked at her solemnly. 'Pursuing you,' he said darkly.

'You're crazy!'

He nodded agreement. 'I must be.'

'What do you want. . . ?'

'I'm coming with you to Ghana,' he said, calmly interrupting her.

'What about your schedule, your commitments?'

'If you remember, I don't have a lecture in Lagos until Tuesday afternoon. Today is Friday. I can go with you to Ghana, deliver you into the hands of Matt and Jackie and catch a plane from Accra to Lagos on Tuesday morning. It's all figured out. I'll get my tickets changed in Accra. The only thing I'm missing is a party at the Ambassador's residence tomorrow night, and I can live without that.' He grinned, looking pleased with himself.

Sanny didn't know what to think or what to say, but she was determined to stay cool. She shrugged casually. 'I can't stop you from coming with me, I suppose, but you're doing it at your own peril.'

'I'll consider myself warned.' There was amusement in his eyes now.

'You may have to eat squid,' she threatened darkly.

'It's delicious,' he said, looking not in the least put off. 'A true delicacy.'

'Oh, it is?'

'Definitely. I've had it before.'

The problem was she had not. It had been available to her once, but she'd been lucky to have had an alternative choice. If they'd find it on the way now he'd probably make her eat it. She groaned inwardly.

'I'm going to check out. Mind if I leave my bag here?' She marched over to the desk, paid her bill and handed back her key. The most important thing was to keep control of herself from now on and not let her emotions carry her along as if she were nothing but a piece of driftwood. She would enjoy his company, but that was where it would have to stop. She pictured in her mind a gigantic sign, round and red, with STOP! spelled out on it in menacing black.

They took a bus along the coastal road to the border. Time passed quickly with amiable conversation. Sanny was in fine form and she began to relax. Mark talked about his family with loving humour. His father was a chef in a very exclusive restaurant (she should have guessed), and his mother was an aerobics teacher at the local YMCA. His sister was a carpenter and his seventeen-year-old brother wanted to go to clown school and join the circus. It seemed a lively family, and she felt a pang of jealousy. She'd grown up in foster-families that had never really been her own.

'Tell me about your family,' he invited, asking the inevitable question.

'I don't have one,' she said lightly. 'I'm a poor little orphan, all alone in the world—I think, anyway. What's that woman carrying on her head?' She pointed outside.

He ignored that. 'What do you mean, you *think*?'

'I think what? Oh. Actually I'm not sure about my father. He left my mother and me when I was three months old. I was told he couldn't stand my crying at night. I got on his nerves. I have no idea where he is.' She sighed. 'Maybe he's rich and famous. Maybe he's dead.'

All through her childhood she'd had dreams and fantasies about her father reappearing—rich and

famous, and he would take her back with him to live in
his enormous mansion with servants all over the place,
and a swimming pool and tennis courts in the back.
And of course he had married some luscious female
who was dying to be her devoted mother and make up
to her all the cruelties life had bestowed on her.
Naturally she would have to forgive her father for
leaving her when she was only a baby, but he would
explain to her his reasons and how hard it had been for
him to do, and they would cry in each other's arms
and all would be well.

'And your mother?' queried Mark.

'My mother died when I was thirteen.'

'I'm sorry.'

'I'm not.' She looked outside. 'See that little girl?
Carrying a baby on her back and a pan of oranges on
her head. She can't be more than six. It always amazes
me how soon they have to grow up and help Mama
out.' She glanced back at him when he didn't answer,
and noticed the dark, thoughtful look in his eyes as he
observed her in silence. She wondered if she'd
shocked him with the comment about her mother's
death, but she didn't want to talk about it now.

She smiled at him brightly. 'I'm beginning to get
hungry. How about you?'

They decided to stay the night in a fishing village near
the beach, rather than in one of the larger towns of
Takoradi and Sekondi. Right on the beach was a
resort enterprise in struggling decline consisting of
some twenty cottages, a small (empty) bar, a
restaurant, and a building with some motel-type
rooms. The place looked deserted, but was open for
business. The buildings were weatherbeaten and the
paint was peeling, but the view was spectacular—a
sandy stretch of palm-covered beach and an endless
ocean with restless foamy waves. They rented a

cottage close to the water, rather than separate rooms
which were in the back and had not much of a view.

It had been a long exhausting day. Having deposited
their luggage in the cottage, they went out for a quick
swim which was wonderfully refreshing. Afterwards
they lay on a towel in the fading light of late afternoon.
Sanny closed her eyes, trying not to picture in her
mind Mark's magnificent muscled body in the black
swimming trunks. He had already been in the water
when she had come out of the cottage and she had
been uncomfortably aware of his eyes on her as she
dashed across the sand and into the waves. She had a
perfectly respectable swimsuit, a fashionable one-
piece, but she felt naked under his regard.

He had followed her as she swum away from him
and he had taken her around the waist and pulled her
to him. She kicked and spluttered.

'Hey! What do you think you're doing?'

'I just want to tell you you're gorgeous.'

'I know. Now let me go before I drown!'

'You won't drown. I'm holding you.'

He sure was. Sanny could feel his long torso along
the whole length of her, feel her breasts pressing
against his chest, her thighs against his. It was
distinctly disturbing, to say the least. Wet skin against
wet skin, his eyes looking into hers, his mouth close to
hers.

It was a very salty kiss, quick but very exciting, and
then he let her go and she swam off wondering if ever
she would breathe normally again, if ever her heart
would calm down.

She lay on her stomach, cheek on her folded arms,
and peeped at him through her lashes. He was looking
at her. His face broke into a grin. So he knew she was
watching him. She turned her face the other way and
heard him laugh. Then there was the feel of his hand
on her bare back and a quiver ran through her.

'You know what I'd like?' he whispered close to her ear.

'Yes. And you can forget it.'

He heaved a heavy sigh. 'That'll be very difficult with you lying there stretched out in all your glory.'

'You could try looking the other way,' she suggested.

'You're very cruel,' he sighed.

'Only when I have to be.'

His hand was slowly stroking her back, softly, sensuously. If he kept that up much longer she'd cave in in no time.

'Move your hand. No hanky-panky,' she said lightly.

He did not oblige. Sanny turned over and sat up, and his hand slid off into the sand.

'You're no fun,' he said petulantly.

'You didn't have to come along with me,' she said reasonably. 'I'm sorry I'm such a disappointment, truly.' She leaped to her feet. 'I'm going in to get dressed. There's no lock on that bedroom door, but I trust you not to play dirty tricks.' She turned and staggered off through the sand, feeling his eyes on her back.

What am I going to do? she asked herself shakily. What am I going to do about myself?

After both of them were dressed they discussed dinner possibilities.

'The cook told me,' said Mark, 'that he can fix us fish and chips English style, with chips made from yams rather than potatoes because they're not available, and a salad, which we should decline no matter what. Or we can have Ghana *chop*, the dish of the day being groundnut stew with chicken. Or we can walk down to where they're bringing in the fish, buy some lobster and he'll prepare that for us.' He grinned. 'That sums up our choices. You take your pick and I'll go along.'

'Let's walk down the beach and watch the fishermen bring in their catch. That will give us something to do at the same time.' Something safe and public, Sanny added silently.

They strolled along on the hard sand near the water's edge in companionable silence. Such a lovely, lonely beach, she thought. No gaudy striped beach umbrellas here, no transistor radios filling the air with rock music, no ice cream vendors, no hotdog stands. Only pure yellow sand, tall coconut palms and an endless sky. Here and there lay old coconut husks and pieces of driftwood, but no empty beer cans or candy wrappers.

Give it time, she thought cynically. If the economy would improve enough to develop some decent accommodation, honest-to-God tourists would not be far behind, bringing with them all the luxuries of beer cans, candy wrappers, and beach umbrellas.

She glanced at Mark, who seemed lost in thoughts of his own. Hands in the pockets of his shorts, he moved his body in leisurely fashion, long bare brown legs strolling at a lazy pace. Sanny took a deep breath, taking in salty air, smelling sea and sunwarmed sand. I'm in love with him, she thought helplessly. I can't look at him or I lose my mental balance. He's sexy and funny and good to be with. He doesn't take himself too seriously.

She hated men who took themselves too seriously, who were so convinced of their own importance, their own superiority. She hated men who were arrogant, patronising and condescending. Mark did not fit any of these categories. He was his own man, secure in himself and not out to impress anybody. And he was male ... definitely very, very male in every possible way.

She liked his easy, relaxed manner. She'd always liked men who had the ability to hang loose, to lie back. Men who didn't make issues out of details, didn't fuss and weren't particular about unimportant things. Sanny had once known a man who was forever combing his hair, straightening his tie and retying his shoes. In her apartment he adjusted the pictures on the wall and the cushions on the couch. When he sat down to eat, he meticulously aligned his knife and fork before picking them up. By the end of the evening she had been ready and sorely tempted to put arsenic in his coffee. She'd wondered how he would behave in bed and had decided that she had absolutely, positively no desire to find out.

They arrived at the scene just as the gigantic net was pulled up on to the sand. It was a pathetic sight. Not more than thirty, maybe forty pounds of fish lay squirming and writhing in the bottom of the huge net that could have contained hundreds of pounds easily.

'My God,' exclaimed Sanny, 'they've been out all night and day, and that's what they get. It's barely enough to feed their own families!'

'It doesn't look very impressive,' Mark agreed. When someone offered to sell them some lobsters, he paid the asking price without even the customary haggling. A small girl put the live lobsters in a flat pan on her head and walked back with them and delivered them to the cook.

Surprisingly, they were not the only ones eating. Apparently the place was not quite as deserted as it had seemed at first sight. There were several people in the open dining area which was cool and breezy and had a view of the beach and the sea.

They were invited to join a couple of Peace Corps volunteers sitting at a large table and were soon joined by some more young people—a Norwegian volunteer who sat on his knees at the table because of a back problem, and an Australian adventurer who had been robbed while sleeping on the beach. He had been left with only the jeans and shirt he was wearing and the wallet in his back pocket. He seemed to take it rather philosophically. At another table an Italian-speaking couple were engaged in a rather animated conversation, gesturing enthusiastically.

All in all, it made for an interesting dinner, and afterwards they all sat around lazily, talking more, enjoying each other's company. In a way it surprised Sanny that Mark seemed to fit in well with this odd assortment of people, but on the other hand maybe it was not so strange. His easy, relaxed manner made people instantly comfortable in his presence—any kind of people.

Leaving the dining area some time later, they found the beach in total darkness, until slowly their eyes became used to it and started distinguishing shapes of palms and cottages.

Mark had taken her hand and they trotted through the dry sand until they came upon a large log not far from their cottage.

'Let's sit here for a while,' he said, lowering himself on to the dry, weathered tree trunk. Sanny sat down beside him and for a while they watched the waves roll in in silence, hearing the calming splashing of water, seeing in the moonlight the odd greenish shine of the luminescent waves.

Such a peaceful place, she thought, not really feeling peaceful at all. Mark, sitting next to her in the dark, had a positively destabilising effect on her, and it was a constant effort to keep her behaviour cool and casual.

'Tell me about your mother,' he said unexpectedly.

It took a moment to let the words sink in. Talking about her mother was the very last thing she wanted to do right now. It was the very last thing she wanted to do at any time.

'My mother is a very unromantic subject of

conversation,' she said casually. 'It's a beautiful night. There are other things to talk about.'

'Don't you like talking about your mother?'

'Not if I can help it. What's that greenish light in the water?'

'Why weren't you sorry when she died?' Mark persisted.

'Aren't you a professor of economics?' she asked pleasantly. 'If you're interested in psychiatry you should have warned me.'

'I'm interested in you, what makes you tick, what makes you say certain things.' He sounded perfectly calm.

'Mostly I say things off the top of my head. You should know that by now.' She smiled brightly. 'Don't make too much of me, don't take me too seriously. I don't myself.'

There was a short silence. 'The greenish light,' he said then, 'is phosphorus in the water. It lights up when the moonshine catches the particles.'

'It looks eerie.' She dug her toes into the sand. Underneath it was cold. She wished he hadn't asked her about her mother. When she had died Sanny had felt no sorrow, no grief, only anger. Anger because it was too late now—too late for her to be adopted and become part of a real family. Nobody wanted to adopt a thirteen-year-old in the throes of puberty. She'd hated her mother for never signing the papers that would have freed her for adoption. After a kind social worker had taken her away from her, her mother had never once really tried to get her back to take care of her again.

It was just as well, she thought bitterly. She'd been underfed, neglected and scared, all her mother's welfare cheque going into drink. Foster-families had taken care of her well enough, but having changed from one family to another several times, she had never felt a sense of belonging, a sense of permanency, a sense of true, unconditional love.

I'm not going to sit here on a romantic African beach and depress myself, she thought suddenly. It's all done and over with. I'm a big girl now, responsible for my own life and my own happiness. There's an exciting man sitting inches away from me. What else do I want?

Turning slightly, she reached for his hand in the dark. It grasped hers, curling warm around her fingers, and his eyes looked directly into hers. His mouth moved into a smile and his head bent to hers.

Sanny leapt into life at his touch like a smouldering fire bursting into flames inside of her. His lips were firm and persuasive and she opened up to him, abandoning all reserve. It was an answering from within, not just from her body, but from a deeper, inner part of herself that she had thought was beyond any reach.

It was not. But tonight she pushed away the fear and the warnings and she let herself go, kissing him with a hungry yearning, feeling his feverish reaction to her responses. She felt herself swept away into some glorious, intoxicating delirium, aware only of the sensuous touches of his mouth on her eyes and cheeks and mouth, of his hands sliding under her shirt and stroking her bare back. Mark drew back slightly and she opened her eyes to look into his face, feeling his hands move forward, touching her bare breasts, caressing them while his eyes looked into hers. A quiver ran through her and she closed her eyes. He drew her to him then, holding her tightly, very tightly until she could feel herself relax in his arms, but it seemed a long, long time.

'Sanny,' he said in a strange, husky voice, 'you'd better know what you're doing if you get me to the brink of insanity again. I'm only human, you know.'

'Why did you stop?' she whispered.

It was silent for a moment. 'I don't know,' he said then. 'I really don't know.'

'It must be the sand,' she said, laughing softly, feeling herself in control again. 'Making love in the sand must be the most uncomfortable, scratchy, gritty exercise there is.'

He groaned, then laughed. '*Exercise*. The words you use!'

'It's my profession—using words, that is.'

'Will you let me read some of your writing?'

'Sure. I have copies of the columns I've sent in to my paper. The only thing I don't want to hear is negative criticism—I'm very bad about that. I don't take it well. I only want to hear words of praise, deserved or not.'

Mark grinned. 'I'll try my very best.'

'All right. I'll fish them out before I go to bed and I'll give them to you tomorrow morning.'

'Why don't we stay here tomorrow?' he asked. 'There's no hurry. We can make Accra on Sunday.'

Staying here for another day would be wonderful and fraught with danger and she knew she shouldn't. Still, she seemed unable to make a reply, positive or negative, and she remained silent.

'It's quiet here,' he continued. 'We can be together for the day, swim, talk. . .'

Make love, she thought, her heart leaping. He was sitting with his arms still around her. I can't, she thought. I'm not ready. I want to, but I'm not ready.

'We can be together and talk on the bus, or on a lorry,' she said evenly.

'Right along with the market mammies with their babies and their chickens and their smoked hogfeet. I want to be alone with you, in a place like this—ocean

breezes, clean air, a deserted beach, palm trees ...
stars at night.'

'You sound terribly romantic,' she said, laughing
softly.

'Only sometimes. I'm no good on a smelly old bus.'
He began to kiss her softly, seductively, but with a
strength that came from somewhere outside herself,
she pulled away.

'No more hanky-panky,' she said airily. 'I want to
go in now and make myself a nice glass of cold milk.'

He groaned. 'You've got to be kidding.'

'Nope, not in the least. The cook said he keeps
boiled water in the refrigerator for us weakling
foreigners, so I'll see if I can have a glass.' She jumped
to her feet, took one step in the dry, loose sand and
promptly lost her balance and went down.

'You deserved that,' Mark said nastily.

She scrambled up. 'May all your camels die in a
blizzard,' she retorted in a fake Arabic accent. As
she trotted off through the sand she heard his
laughter following her. He was next to her a moment
later.

'I'll escort you so you won't get molested in this
dark and dangerous place.'

'Fat chance! But I admire your gallantry. You're a
true gentleman.'

He heaved a martyred sigh. 'Why do I have the
feeling that I'd have more fun if I weren't quite so
noble and chivalrous?'

'I have no idea, but don't give it up.'

With the exception of her swimsuit all her clothes
were missing the next morning when she woke up. For
a fleeting moment she thought of the Australian
adventurer. Had she joined the ranks of the robbed?
No.

Mark had taken them, it was obvious. Well, she

thought dryly, wavering between anger and laughter, we mourn the loss of one more gentleman.

So he wanted them to stay here for another day. It certainly wouldn't be the worst thing that had ever happened to her, but the idea of falling victim to Mark's wishes and whims went quite against the grain of her personality. Now what?

She sat on the edge of the bed, staring vacantly at the ashes of a mosquito coil that had burned itself out during the night. Ranting and raving would have no effect on him, so she might as well forget that and not give him the satisfaction. Trying to find her clothes would be useless. He'd have stashed them away where she'd never find them, or couldn't get to them. He'd probably paid the cook's wife to keep them in her house, or whatever.

There was no choice but to stay the day, she might as well accept that fact. But Mark wasn't going to get what he thought he would. His evil schemes weren't going to pay off, she would make sure of that.

Her stomach growled inelegantly. She wondered if he expected her to have breakfast in her nightgown or in her swimsuit. She'd better find out. She put on her swimsuit.

She discovered him on the beach, stretched out in the sun, brown body glistening with water, hair soaked.

'Had a nice swim?' she asked, sitting down next to him in the sand.

'Superb.' He half-opened his eyes to look at her. 'Did you sleep well?'

'Like a rock, as you must have seen for yourself.'

'Right.'

'I thought you were a gentleman,' Sanny said evenly.

'I gave it up.'

'Taking away my clothes ... cheap, cheap tactics.'

'I tried charm, romance and seduction and it didn't get me anywhere.'

Silence. She was going to take this cool and calm. She was going to be classy and civilised all the way.

'What are your plans for breakfast?' she asked, squinting against the bright morning sun. 'I have some stale bread in my bag and a can of sardines, but. . . .'

'Breakfast will be delivered to our cottage by special order. Scrambled eggs, toast and fresh pineapple.'

'Sounds wonderful.'

'A lot better than sardines,' Mark agreed.

She let her eyes wander over his long lean body stretched out on the blue towel. There was some light curly hair on his chest, a shade darker than that on his head. She had the urge to run her hand over it and through it, but it was not an impulse she intended to give in to at this time. His face was calm, square chin relaxed, eyes closed. His features were strong but irregular giving him that unfinished look she found somehow very attractive.

He opened his eyes, catching hers. 'What are you looking at?'

'You. Your eyebrows are crooked.'

'Thanks. That's what I need on an empty stomach.' He sat up and gave her a hard, appraising stare. 'Your mouth is too wide,' he said coldly.

Sanny grinned. 'That's from smiling so much.'

'Too much.' He jumped up, reached for her hand and pulled her up. 'Breakfast is just arriving.'

His comment stuck in her mind, repeating itself over and over, and it irritated her. Too much. Too much. Too much. She smiled too much—what did he mean by that? What did he want her to do? Cry? Yell? Take everything he said seriously? Get mad at every little excuse? Forget it. She'd rather laugh. She'd rather smile.

Breakfast over, she sat down at the rickety table, now cleared of dishes, and began to write.

'Working?' he enquired casually.

'Gotta earn my daily *chop*,' she answered, trying out the local word for food.

'You have those columns handy?'

She shook her head. 'They're at the bottom of the bag with my clothes in it. The one that you absconded with,' she clarified, as if he might have forgotten. Absently she chewed at the end of her felt-tip pen.

'I'll read them tomorrow, then,' Mark said easily, picking up a paperback novel and settling in a chair nearby.

'I do hope you stashed my stuff some place safe.' Her eyes were on the notebook in front of her as if the words she was speaking did not deserve her full attention.

'Quite safe.'

'I'd hate to think I'd have to go to the local market in my swimsuit and buy back my own clothes, or to see one of the cleaning girls sashaying in here wearing my only pair of jeans,' she added.

'You haven't a thing to worry about.'

She made a pretence of writing. 'That's a load off my mind,' she said abstractedly.

'I thought it might be.'

Sanny would have gladly poured a cup of coffee over his head, but not having one handy she had to give up that idea. She was going to play it cool. He wouldn't get a rise out of her.

She began to write in earnest now, checking the notes she'd made the day before. They were skimpy owing to the distraction of a charming, amusing male sitting next to her in the bus and due to the fact that she'd paid too much attention to him and not enough to what was going on around her. But yesterday's events were still fresh in her mind and working them out now was the smartest thing to do. Good too because it excluded Mark.

'What are you writing about?' he asked.

'Yesterday. About the rubber plantation and the coconut oil mill we saw in the village where we had lunch,' she said patiently, determined not to get irked.

'You mean that smelly operation under the thatched roof?'

'Yeah. What would you call it?' She turned and looked at him with feigned interest.

Mark frowned as if deep in thought. 'A coconut oil mill.'

'Brilliant!'

He grinned. 'They didn't make me a professor for nothing.'

'That's good to know. Do you mind if I work for a while?' she asked pleasantly.

'Not at all. By all means, work for a while,' his tone matched hers perfectly. He lowered his eyes to his book and Sanny turned back to her work.

It was quiet for about an hour. Really quiet. He said not a word, not one. Sanny began to wonder about it until she finally heard him get up. She kept her eyes glued to her notebook.

'I think I'll go for a stroll. It looks nice out there.'

'Mmm,' she muttered, not looking up.

'See you later.'

He was gone. She saw him tramping off through the sand to the water's edge. It did look wonderful out there with the waves splashing on to the beach and the palms swaying in the ocean breeze. He hadn't even asked if she wanted to come along—phooee to him! She felt piqued without wanting to.

Heaving a sigh of resignation, she went back to work. She hated writing longhand, but the chance of getting hold of a typewriter here was nil. She'd have to wait till she got to Accra. Maybe she could borrow one from the Simmonses for a few hours.

Mark was back half an hour later, carrying a pineapple which he started attacking with his Swiss army knife as soon as he sat down again on the verandah. Juice dripped down his fingers. He held out a chunk for her.

'Want a piece?'

'Thanks.' She took it from him. It was sweet and deliciously refreshing. Sanny licked her fingers, not caring that he saw her do it, and pushed her notebook aside with her elbows.

'I'm quitting,' she announced. 'I've done enough for a while.'

'Good. You deserve a break. Here, have another piece.'

Between the two of them they devoured the entire pineapple.

'Look at us,' she said, 'we're disgusting. No couth, no manners.'

'Yeah,' he smirked, 'ain't it great?'

Her mind produced an instant picture of Mark in his sophisticated lightweight suit in the classy comfort of the exclusive restaurant where they had eaten in Abidjan. Now he was sitting across from her in a faded pair of denim shorts, his feet in rubber thongs, his chest bare, and his hands dripping with pineapple juice. He certainly had digressed. He even looked as if he was enjoying it.

They raced each other to the sea to take a swim and wash off the juice that had found its way from hands to knees and legs. Mark hadn't bothered to change into his swimming trunks and went right in wearing his shorts. They would probably take all of fifteen minutes to dry again, so he probably didn't find it worth the effort, she thought. Professor of Economics. If she hadn't heard and seen him give a lecture, and if she hadn't seen him in his other incarnation, she wouldn't have believed it.

He didn't touch her at all in the water, which actually surprised her, she admitted to herself. They lay down on their towels in the full sun to dry off and she had almost dozed off listening to the sounds of water and waves and the birds somewhere out in the trees when a gentle, ticklish sensation on her thigh made her open her eyes and chased the sleepiness away. Mark was trailing his finger up the outside of her thigh until it came to rest right at the edge of her swimsuit.

'What's this?' he asked, increasing the pressure of his finger.

She watched him through her lashes. 'A tattoo. You know, one of those things sailors have on their arms and chests.' The one she had on her thigh was a minuscule little heart and arrow with an 'S' at one end and a 'P' at the other.

'You were a sailor once?'

'Almost. I tried to stow away on a ship when I was sixteen.'

Mark surveyed her through half-closed lids. 'Interesting. You have to tell me about that some time.'

'Sure. Whenever.'

'What does the "P" stand for?'

'Peter. Look at that ship on the horizon. It's a big one.'

'Who's Peter?'

CHAPTER FOUR

'I DON'T remember.' Sanny peered at the boat. 'Do you think it's a fishing boat? Somebody was telling me that Starkist in California has a Japanese fleet fishing for tuna here off the coast of Africa and that they carry the fish to Puerto Rico for canning and that the stuff never sees California. Do you think it's true?'

'Why not? Who's Peter?' Mark repeated.

'I told you, I don't remember.' She had certainly tried hard enough to forget.

'You mean to tell me,' he said in patient tones, 'that you had Peter tattooed on your thigh but you don't remember him?'

'I think he was my boy-friend,' she prevaricated.

'What happened?'

She gave an exasperated sigh. 'What do you think happened? He went away to college, fell for a cheerleader—blonde, blue-eyed and five foot eight— got her pregnant, married her and divorced her.'

'Of course, I should have guessed. How did you feel about that?'

'I thought to myself, better her than me.'

She had lost six pounds in three weeks crying into her food and spending sleepless nights cursing him. He had left her, like everybody else had always left her. He had stopped loving her. He had found someone else, someone tall and blonde and blue-eyed, all the things she was not. She'd thought their love was for ever. It was going to be the first thing in her life that was going to be permanent. She'd felt so sure and so confident about that. The tattoo had been her way of expressing that confidence. Now she would

72

have to live with it till the end of her days, or until she'd get courage enough to get plastic surgery and have it made un-permanent. Until then it would serve her as a reminder of her own idiocy, her romantic illusions. Nothing was permanent.

'Why did you decide to have a tattoo done?' Mark asked.

'Because I was sixteen and stupid. And because I wanted it. And because they told me I wasn't allowed to do it.' She'd been wild, willful and rebellious in her teenage years.

'Who are "they"?'

'The people I was living with at the time.' Sanny turned over on her back and stared up into the sky. They'd been nice people and they'd tried hard, but by then it was too late.

'Relatives?'

'No. I have no relatives that I know of. They were just people who'd taken me in out of the goodness of their heart. And I wish you'd stop third-degreeing me!' she finished crossly.

'How else am I going to find out anything about you?' he asked reasonably. 'You're sure not too loose with the information.'

'Because it's very uninteresting.'

'That's not for you to decide, is it?'

'I find this conversation extremely boring.' She sat up, raking sandy fingers through her wet curls. 'Yuk! I'm going inside and rinse out my hair.'

Which was easier said than done. The shower spray demonstrated a distinct lack of gusto and it took a while before she had sand and salt sufficiently eliminated from her hair.

They had fish and yam chips at the little restaurant—beautiful white flaky fish and dry, crusty chips. It all had a slightly sweet flavor. Like much of the food Sanny had eaten on her travels, it was fried in coconut oil that had not been refined to the greatest degree of purity. She thought again of the oil extraction plant she had seen in one of the villages on the way over. It was interesting to see people working in such small-scale, grass roots enterprises. People seemed to know and understand their jobs as having some reality, which was something hard to find in screwing anonymous pieces into anonymous parts of anonymous products in assembly plants. The owner of the oil extraction plant was a very enterprising individual who had started the business with next to nothing and was now employing a considerable percentage of the village population which was very beneficial for its economy, needless to say.

Sanny had found a lot of this entrepreneurial spirit in the places she had visited, a lot of it demonstrated by women, too. She had been very surprised by the liberated role the women in West Africa were playing in economic situations. She was going to do a big article on that, she'd already decided. A special folder was set up in which everything pertaining to women and their lives was filed away.

She had eaten her lunch wearing her swimsuit covered by a T-shirt that had been left on a chair in her room. She had been grateful for that, because she had no desire to do any begging for her clothes. Fortunately this was a very casual place and judging from the odd assortment of garments the other people were wearing, nobody would give a hoot about hers.

Walking back to the cottage she considered working some more—she really needed to think about another column—but she felt terribly lazy and gave up the idea. Taking sunglasses and a paperback novel, she settled herself in the shade of the coconut palms in front of the cottage and began to read. Mark, apparently, had had the same idea and was reading too. Good—maybe she could have some peace and quiet. His interest in her was getting a little too disturbing. She didn't want to have him ask her any more questions if she could help it.

She felt lazy and lethargic. Feeling drowsiness steal over her, she closed her eyes and decided not to fight it. She dozed for a while, and when she opened her eyes again, Mark was gone. She saw him walk towards the sea with easy, fluid movements and the lean brown fitness of him tugged at her senses. It had not been easy today, trying to stay cool and composed in such close proximity to him. She was acutely aware of him every single moment—aware of the vital, virile attractiveness of that bronzed, muscular body dressed only in shorts. He was wearing his black swimming trunks now, she noticed, watching him as she started wading into the water.

Should she follow him in? It would wake her up, that much was sure. His head was disappearing behind the waves. She hoped he wouldn't do anything foolish—the undercurrents were treacherous.

Having made up her mind, she struggled clumsily to her feet and stripped the T-shirt off over her head. The water was wonderfully refreshing. Not being a strong swimmer she didn't venture out too far, but she kept an eye out for Mark. He was suddenly next to her, like an apparition from the waves, startling her.

'Didn't mean to scare you,' he said, swinging wet hair out of his eyes with a swift movement of his head. 'Had a nice sleep?'

Sanny grinnned. 'I'm trying to wake myself up. I haven't been so lazy for weeks, and I'm almost feeling guilty.'

'Don't. When you're ready to come out we'll have a cold beer. How does that sound?'

'Like a miracle,' she returned dryly. 'According to our volunteer friends, beer hasn't been available for months.'

'Given the right economic incentives,' Mark told her, 'someone will come up with a couple of bottles. I sent out a search party this morning.'

'You're devious,' she said, laughing, and swam away.

Beer there was, and even cold, four bottles in all. It tasted like champagne to her thirsty body. It probably had cost the price of champagne, she thought, but didn't ask.

Shortly before dark Mark returned her bag with clothes, dumping it unceremoniously at her feet.

'Thank you,' she said blandly.

'You know,' he said conversationally, 'I like you better all the time.'

She lifted a quizzical brow. 'You do?'

'You're a good sport,' he told her. 'I appreciate that.'

A good sport? Because she hadn't made a fuss? It would have been useless and unproductive.

'Thank you. But I wouldn't be too hasty with my praise if I were you. My mind's been very busy all day long.' She goggled at him and moved her index finger around in fast circling motions. 'Busy, busy, busy searching for appropriate retaliatory measures.'

His eyes were dancing. 'And what have you come up with?'

'You'll see.' She hadn't come up with anything, but he didn't have to know that. To tell the truth, she'd only given the idea of reprisal a fleeting moment of thought, then given up on it.

'I can't wait.' He was looking down on her with those laughing eyes that made her feel weak like water. It had been a long day—a long day without him ever touching her except for the time he was asking about the tattoo on her thigh. He was too close for comfort. She could feel the warmth of his body radiating on to her own bare skin. He was still bare-chested and she wanted badly to touch him. She wanted very much to put her arms around him and kiss him. The yearning raced like a flame all the way through her.

He'd wanted to stay on for the day, to be alone with her. For what? She had been determined this morning not to give him what she had thought he had been after. He wasn't going to touch her. He wasn't going to play any games with her.

Well, the joke was on her—he hadn't. And what was more, she was standing here wishing he would pull her close and kiss her. And he wasn't.

'What are you thinking about?' His voice was low, and she made herself look right at him. Then slowly she put the palms of her hands flat on his chest and slowly moved them up to his shoulders, then around his neck, pulling his face down to hers.

The blood was throbbing in her ears as she kissed him. He hugged her close, taking command after accepting her initiative with welcoming warmth. Her body sang to his touch, trembling with a longing she had never felt so intensely before. Frightened by her lack of composure, she gently pulled away.

'Am I very forward?' she asked, forcing herself to look at him.

'Very. And I'm enjoying every minute of it.'

'I wanted to do that very much,' she said on a low note, the admission coming without conscious thought.

'I could tell,' Mark returned, dry humour in his voice.

'Only ... I want you to understand that it wasn't meant as an invitation to more and greater thrills.'

His expression didn't change. 'Why not?' he asked softly.

Sanny met his eyes squarely. 'Because I haven't made up my mind about that yet.'

'But not because you don't want to?'

She shook her head. 'I couldn't fool you about that, could I?'

His smile came slow. 'No, you couldn't fool me about that.'

He knew very well how she reacted to him, the impact he had on her. It would be ludicrous to try and deny it. Just standing near him made her pulse race. But this time it was he who took the initiative, drawing her to him and kissing her with a slow, deliberate sensuality that seemed to make every cell of her body tingle with life. He made her feel more alive than anyone had ever done, and the fact that he had that power over her frightened her more than anything. She yearned for the sensations he aroused in her, but they frightened her too. She didn't like the lack of control and composure that was an integral part of those feelings. It left her much too vulnerable.

Again she pulled away. Mark looked at her, his eyes dark. 'You'd better make up your mind fast,' he said huskily. 'I'm not made of stone, you know. Although you must admit I did well keeping my hands off you today. No easy accomplishment with you parading around with next to nothing on.'

'Whose fault was that? I didn't have a choice, did I?'

'I'm talking about fact, not fault,' he countered easily. His hands slid down her hips and came to rest on the bare skin of her thighs. 'You're very nice to look at, even nicer to touch. You'd better put some clothes on before I lose all my cool.' His hands began an upward movement, sliding over her stomach up to her breasts, slowly lowering her swimsuit.

Sanny jerked away, catching the glint in his eyes as she did so.

'I was only trying to help,' he said innocently.

'I know all about that kind of help,' she returned sweetly, then picking up the bag, she swung out the door into her own room and closed the door.

She stripped off the swimsuit and hurried into the shower. Cursing at the ineffectual trickle of water, she washed and rinsed as well as she could, then went in search of something to wear for dinner. They'd walked to the fishermen again that afternoon and bought a batch of huge shrimps which would be prepared for them by the cook. She was ravenous and hoped he would do a good job.

With a sigh of resignation she pulled on her jeans and a shirt. She felt like dressing up and making herself look good. She knew exactly which dress she wanted to wear (black, slinky, sexy), only it was hanging in her closet at home, thousands of miles away. The clothes she had brought with her were designed for comfort and practicality, not for looking seductive and sexually attractive. It was just as well, she thought dryly. Mark didn't need any encouragement—he was doing very well without it.

For a long time she stared at the warm brown glow of her face in the mirror, then picked up a lipstick and put some on. A little mascara and that was all—she was finished. Her hair was curling rather wildly in the humidity and there was little she could do to control it, but it looked all right, so she might as well not worry about it.

The shower was making miserable little splish-splash noises as she passed the bathroom. She sat down in a chair on the little verandah outside and waited for Mark. It was dark already and she stared up into the palm crowns and listened to the small and mysterious noises that came from everywhere around her. The night air was warm, but the burning heat had left with the sun and a soft breeze from the water was rustling the palm fronds. An idyllic place, this.

Mark wasn't married, he'd said. She'd asked him over dinner one night in Abidjan, having no intention or inclination to hang around with a married man, and especially not because she knew she wasn't immune to his charm. If he was married and wanted a fling he'd have to do it with someone else.

Since she was not particularly gullible or naïve, it had crossed her mind that he might be lying. Not being particularly inexperienced and rather well tuned in to listening between the lines, she had soon rejected that possibility. It was always possible that he was a real con man, of course, but her instincts along with the rest of the signs told her she was right—he wasn't lying. He wasn't married.

She wondered why. He certainly seemed to be prime husband material. His female students were probably falling all over him trying to hook him. No wonder he seemed so sure of himself! That kind of reinforcement was vitamin therapy for any man's ego.

So, she thought, what's he chasing me around for?

Because he's fallen head over heels in love with you, her Other Self said.

Sure, sure.

Well, he said so himself.

Which means zero. It's easy enough to say. Most women would be bowled over by such an admission.

But you weren't. You played it nice and cool.

Which I'll keep doing.

If you can.

She probably couldn't. She most certainly couldn't. Mark had a devastating effect on her emotions and self-control. All he had to do was try only a little bit harder and she'd be lost. He could make love to her any old time he wanted to. Didn't he know that?

Of course he knows that! answered her Other Self.

Well, why then is he biding his time? What's he waiting for?

Maybe he's a gentleman and likes mutually-embarked-upon ecstasy only.

He swiped my clothes this morning. He's no gentleman—he said he'd given it up.

Maybe he sees no reward in instant victory. After all, he's an economist. Maybe he's interested in long-range results rather than short-term pay offs.

Yeah, she thought derisively, next thing I know he'll ask me to marry him.

Well, stranger things have happened. It wouldn't be the first time a man asked you to marry him.

She shifted in her chair and sighed, pushing away memories. The man had been a very uninteresting individual who had followed her around in blind adoration—why, she had never understood and never cared to.

From out in the dark someone called her name. The voice was accompanied by a flashlight which seemed to move in the direction of the cottage on its own accord.

Out of the dark emerged Steve, the Aussie adventurer. He enquired politely if she and Mark had had dinner yet, and when she said no, he asked to join them, which was fine by Sanny. At lunch she had asked him if he would mind if she asked him some questions about his travels for possible use in her articles, and he seemed willing enough. He was tall and lanky and had warm brown eyes that were very pleasant to look at, and his accent was a treat to Sanny, who had never met an Australian before.

He sat down next to her to wait for Mark who came out only minutes later and the three of them went to the restaurant in search of food. Mark offered to share the shrimps, which Steve hesitantly but gratefully accepted after it was obvious that there was plenty to go around.

After dinner was over and the dishes were cleared, Sanny took out her notebook and settled down for her questioning. They spent a pleasant couple of hours talking, while Mark watched and listened quietly, never saying a word. He was observing her do her job, she knew. It made her faintly uneasy, but it passed quickly as she got more involved in Steve's stories. He had plenty to tell.

'You're good,' Mark told her as they walked back together.

'Oh, that was easy!' she said, and it was true, of course.

'You're still good,' he returned dryly. His hand was resting lightly on her shoulder.

'Thank you,' she said graciously. 'You were very quiet,' she added.

'It wasn't my turn to talk. Did I make you nervous?'

'Did I look nervous?'

His hand moved up and gently brushed her cheek, then went down on her shoulder again. 'Only a little.' There was a smile in his voice.

'I knew you were observing me, evaluating me. It made me feel funny.'

'Well, you got an A plus,' he assured her.

'Thank you, Professor.'

Not wanting to go back, they took a walk along the beach, talking very little, and it was wonderful and peaceful being with him, her hand in his. It was a very dark night, the moon only a thin sliver in the starry sky. She watched the waves, only the white foamy crests visible, and it seemed all very mysterious and a little bit eerie. Except for the sounds of the sea she heard no other noises and it was easy to imagine they were the only two people on some exotic desert island.

And now, let's be romantic. Sanny almost laughed at herself.

'When's my punishment coming?' Mark asked suddenly, and it took a moment for her to remember what he was talking about.

'You'll have to wait. Suffer a little. You can take it, you're tough, aren't you?'

'As a rock,' he agreed. There was a slight pause. 'But not in everything,' he added then, and she had no trouble at all figuring out what he was alluding to.

'It's nice to know you have a weakness,' she said lightly. 'I hate perfect men, they're so boring.'

'You don't have to worry about that with me,' he assured her. 'I have a couple of nasty streaks in my make up.'

'As I found out this morning when I couldn't find my clothes.'

Mark stopped suddenly, stepping in front of her. He put both his hands on her shoulders, bending his head toward her to look at her face. 'Are you sorry we stayed here today instead of going on?' he asked.

'Actually, I had a very nice, lazy day, which doesn't mean you're off the hook.' She peered into the dark-shadowed face, but couldn't make out his expression. Why was her heart leaping around in her chest again?

'In a way I'm sorry that we did,' he said, his voice oddly low.

'You surprise me. Why?'

The silence seemed to stretch endlessly and she could feel her body begin to tense. His hands moved down her back and he slowly drew her to him.

'Because,' he said in her ear, 'I want you so badly I'm going out of my mind, and I don't know how I'm going to keep my hands off you tonight.'

Try taking a plunge, she thought wildly. You've got the whole Atlantic Ocean at your feet. His words caused such an upwelling of longing for him that she could feel her legs grow weak and panic surged through her. Please, she prayed, stay cool, don't let this happen, don't lose your head.

Why not? Why not, if I want him so much?

Because he'll leave like all the others, answered her

Other Self. Two days from now he'll be in Nigeria, and you'll never see him again.

So I know. I'm prepared for it. It can't hurt me if I know it's coming. He doesn't have to know how I really feel. He has no power over me if he doesn't know.

She swallowed. 'You know I want to,' she said, making her voice level.

'I also know that you haven't made up your mind that you will.'

'And that stops you?' she asked incredulously.

'Yes,' he returned dryly. 'Respecting a woman's wishes, or trying to, never hurt any man.'

She pulled away from him, looking into his eyes. 'You sound so noble, I can't believe my ears!'

Mark laughed then. 'When I was young I learned to my own detriment that seducing a self-respecting female against her inclinations, moral or otherwise, had very few long-term rewards.' His grin showed his teeth, white in the dark. 'Of course, at the time it made me feel all-powerful and terribly macho.'

'One more scalp on your belt, so to speak.'

'Something like that. I suppose men go through a phase like that as a growing experience—proving to themselves and the world they're all male, all man.'

'And you've proved it?'

'Let's say I'm not particularly concerned any more about the way the world views me.'

'And women?' she queried.

'I don't have too much trouble with them, either.'

'I thought not.' Sanny made a move to turn away, but his hands held her back.

'That conversation didn't exactly take the turn I had intended it to,' he said calmly. 'You have a way of doing that.'

'One of my many talents,' she said sassily.

For a moment he stared at her silently. 'All right,'

he said then, 'I suppose we'd better turn back to the mansion.'

Which they did, in silence. Only this time it was not quite so peaceful, not quite so tranquil. There was a tension between them, a crackling in the silence, intangible vibrations in the air.

Mark wasn't holding her hand as they walked on the wet sand and she longed for his touch, tense with suppressed emotion. If he touched her now she'd burst into flames like a torch.

Oh, God, she thought in panic, what's the matter with me? How come I can't do what I've done so many times before—take a step back, look at it in perspective. How come I can't be rational?

In numb concentration she gazed at her bare feet as they squished on the wet sand, leaving behind faint prints. One step after another. One two, one two, one two.

The lights of the cottages came into view and they moved towards them through the dry sand, still without speaking. Mark opened the door and let her in ahead of him, not switching on the light.

'Sanny . . .' There was no question in the way he spoke her name, but she felt his hands as they reached for her in the dark and she came to him without reservation, putting her cheek against his chest. She could feel and hear his heartbeat, and she closed her eyes as a feverish sensation surged through her.

Gentle hands lifted her face and his lips found hers, brushing them with soft sensuality and then retreating almost immediately.

'Goodnight, Sanny.' His voice sounded strange. She thought she was going to die. Her legs were shaking and her mind was in chaos. Her throat was dry and she couldn't produce a sound. Turning without saying a word, she dashed into her room and collapsed on the bed.

He doesn't have to know how I really feel, she thought. If he doesn't know he can't hurt me. As long as I don't believe in fairy tales, I'll be fine. I have no illusions, so nothing can hurt me. Nothing.

In a daze she took off her clothes and wrapped a towel sarong-fashion around herself. Without making a sound she tiptoed out of the room. His door was slightly ajar and she pushed it open all the way and crept in. He stood by the window, hands on his hips, legs slightly apart. He stood staring out over the sea, and she slipped next to him, looking out over the waves for an eternity of silence.

In the stillness she was conscious of her shallow and irregular breathing and the erratic beating of her heart. She knew he was aware of her presence next to him, even though he didn't move and didn't speak. Between them a nameless emotion stirred the air, filled the room. And when finally Mark moved and drew her to him she knew there was no going back.

For a moment his mouth was soft and gentle on hers, then something seemed to break inside him and his kiss became deep and hungry and overpowering. Sanny began to tremble and his arms tightened around her and then she felt herself lifted and then lowered on to the bed. He was with her moments later, gently removing the towel. Feeling his warm bare skin against her own made fire race through her blood. He kissed her again, his hands moving over her body in sensual caresses, stirring in her sensations that were overwhelming and all-consuming. Her response was instinctual, coming from unknown depths, and her body moved to his in a soundless, wordless answering.

CHAPTER FIVE

SHE'D never known it could be like this. She'd never known there could be such true loving passion. She'd never known she could give herself with so much deep, intense emotion.

She lay in Mark's arms in the dark and silent room, bewildered by the feelings unleashed in her, the all-consuming fire that had sprung up from some deep and secret part of her. Only he had been capable of bringing it out, only he had had the power of obliterating in her consciousness everything except the feelings and sensations he evoked in her. Such warm and wild and wondrous loving she had never known.

Lying in his arms, she held her face close against his, holding him so tight her arms ached, and she was grateful for his silence, because one word and she would burst into tears.

He began to stroke her hair in slow, soothing motions over and over, then one hand slid down her bare back and caressed her in soft, calming movements until she could feel herself grow quiet and tranquil. A peace stole over her.

In her mind there were no words, only feelings of deep and tender gratitude, of joy and loving and fulfilment, and she closed her eyes, slipping away into sleep with a sigh of contentment.

When she awoke she was still in his arms. His body, relaxed in sleep, was warm and heavy against her. A surge of such joyous loving rushed through her that her heart leapt in response. For endless minutes she gazed into his sleeping face, seeing every line and angle of his features, searching for she knew not what.

Slowly she lowered her mouth to his, brushing her lips gently against his and he gave a soft moan. He stirred and opened his eyes, looking directly into hers.

A knowing smile chased the sleepiness from his expression and with a groan he hugged her to him. 'Mmm . . . some way to wake up!'

'You're a superb lover,' Sanny whispered in his ear. 'Just in case you didn't know.'

'Mmm . . . we strive to please.'

'You did.'

'I could tell,' he said, humour in his voice. 'I had no trouble telling at all.'

Her face was buried in his neck and she was acutely aware of the warm, intimate smell of him, feeling his skin against her mouth and nose and cheek, a most delightful, sensual closeness. She moved her lips against him, touched his skin with her tongue, feeling his immediate, intense reaction. She wanted him then with such a sudden burst of fierce longing that the impact of it trembled through her like a shock. For a moment she lay against him without breathing, feeling his hands touching her again with gentle urgency, then taking in a deep ragged breath she gave herself up once more to the overwhelming force of magical emotions sweeping through her.

The morning light seemed too bright and revealing when her senses returned, and she hid her face from his view. Spent and exhausted, she tried to calm down, to please, please appear to have some semblance of cool and composure.

'What's the matter?' he whispered, kissing the back of her neck.

'Nothing,' she muttered into the pillow. Nothing except that I'm overcome with those stormy, tumultuous, chaotic emotions I don't know how to handle and I don't want you to see me in this state. You opened something up inside me and I feel exposed and fragile, and if you'd look into my face you'd see. And I can't let you see. . . .

'Look at me, Sanny,' he whispered, his mouth against her ear, his hands moving through her hair. 'I want to see you. Tell me how you feel.'

She shook her head, her face rubbing the pillow. 'It's too light. It hurts my eyes.' Her words were muffled sounds and she wasn't sure he had heard her, but he was silent then, kissing her softly, gently pulling her curls and winding them around his fingers, playing.

It took a while before she felt composed enough to face him and she turned around on her back, smiling serenely up at him. His eyes were full of gentle laughter. He bent to kiss her nose.

'Welcome back,' he said softly. Sanny had a sudden fearful feeling that maybe he knew what was deep inside her, that maybe he knew what confusion he had wrought in her, what secret part of her he had unearthed.

'You're a miracle worker,' she said lightly.

'It takes two, you know.' He took one of her hands and kissed her fingers one by one, his eyes not leaving her face. 'And it helps if there's something here.' He placed her hand on his chest over his heart. 'Something special, something good.'

'You're such a romantic,' she murmured.

'Incurable. We'd be drinking champagne, except that it seems a bit out of the question here.'

'We do have those two extra bottles of beer we didn't drink,' she said, straightfaced.

Mark gave her a long, dark look. 'Beer in bed. It doesn't do a thing for me. No romance in you, is there?'

She raised her brows, looking innocent. 'Powdered milk? Nice and cold?'

He groaned. 'I'm getting up. You sure know how to chase a man out of bed.' He jumped up, and she watched as the sunlight streamed over his smooth brown body and her heart gave a curious leap and her throat went dry.

I love him, she thought.

The inevitable implications were paralysing, and for a moment she couldn't breathe.

The first man she had ever loved was Daddy David. She'd been four years old and terrified when she had been taken away from her mother to the house of Auntie Ann and Daddy David. There were two pictures of her dating back to that time. She'd been skinny and undernourished, with huge dark eyes in a little white face surrounded by a mop of wild dark curls.

The first few days she had cried for her mother. She had not understood why she couldn't stay with her any longer. She had started to understand better when she became used to the routine of a normal household with a loving family. There were three other children of whom two were also foster-children. The oldest son was a 'real' son, even though that word was never used to describe him. To Auntie Ann and Daddy David they were all real and they were all loved.

Daddy David started out being Uncle David, but Sanny, who had dreamed of a daddy as long as she could remember and prayed fervently for one every night, wanted him to be a daddy. So first it had changed to Uncle Daddy, until finally it stuck on Daddy David. God had answered her prayers.

He had been a warm, loving man who carried her around on his shoulders and helped her build sand castles on the beach and taught her how to ride a bicycle.

As she grew to be five and six and seven, the

pictures showed her to be a happy, laughing child, no longer hungry-looking—cared for, loved.

When she was seven, Daddy David became seriously ill and her whole life crumbled around her. Daddy David would not recover. Auntie Ann did what she could, but the 'Higher Authorities' had better ideas for the foster-children; they were removed from the household. Different, happier homes would be found for them. Sanny's misery was acute. Why could she not stay with the people who loved her? She could help take care of Daddy David while he was ill. She *wanted* to take care of Daddy David. She loved him. He was the only father she had ever known. How could they take her away from him?

They could and they did. She was delivered to another family, like a package, with her clothes and her toys bundled up in a red suitcase and a variety of plastic bags advertising department stores. She would stay with them only temporarily, it was explained to her, until they had found her a suitable family who would take her in on a long-term basis.

Temporarily turned out to be more than a year, a terribly unhappy year. She worried about Daddy David. They wouldn't let her visit him, even though she didn't live more than twenty miles away from her former foster-family. The social worker didn't want to talk about him, not really. It seemed to Sanny that she was supposed to forget him and concentrate on happier thoughts, but it was impossible to do so.

Out of necessity she had had to change schools, and it had been difficult to adjust because right along with her family she'd also lost all her friends.

There was only one other child in the family beside herself—a teenage boy with pimples and red hair who played the guitar and sang melancholy love songs. The people were kind to her, but she lacked the feeling of being loved. They had a dog of gargantuan proportions with a wolfish appearance who scared her out of her wits. She spent many lonely hours in her room, avoiding the dog, and writing in a notebook about the things that had happened to her during the day and her worries about Auntie Ann and Daddy David. Nobody else wanted to hear about them and it was a relief to get it all out of her system by writing it down.

She started wondering about her own mother and her own father—the one who had run away from them. Her mother had said, in one of her less-sober moments, that he couldn't stand Sanny crying at night. She was colicky and always crying, for hours on end. It was her fault that her father had left. She should have known better and shut up at night so he could get his sleep, but she hadn't known better because she'd only been a little baby. She began to blame herself, even though there seemed to be something very unfair about that.

Her mother had come to see her only one time after she had been taken away at the age of four. After that she only sent cards or presents for her birthday and Christmas. They were always wrong—the wrong size, the wrong colour, the wrong type of toys (too childish or too sophisticated), or they arrived too late. Apparently her mother wasn't always sure whether Sanny's birthday was in June or July.

Two months after the fact Sanny was told of Daddy David's death. It was soon after she had been moved to the 'long-term' family, and she had cried her heart out for a week straight. They should have told her. She hadn't even had a chance to see him one last time and tell him how much she loved him.

Auntie Bertha, the new aunt, had seen her distress, pulled her on to her voluminous lap as if she were still a small child, and made her tell all. Finally somebody wanted to hear. The words had come pouring out accompanied by torrents of tears—fourteen months' worth of pent-up distress. It was such a relief to let it all out, Sanny felt reborn when it was over.

Aunt Bertha was the size of a battleship, but soft and warm and motherly, and she smelled of vanilla, which happened to be Sanny's favourite flavour for almost anything—ice cream, pudding, cake. Sitting on Aunt Bertha's lap that night, face against her ample bosom, soaking the material of her dress and smelling the vanilla, was a treasured memory. Aunt Bertha had earned her undying love.

Uncle Nick was not at all like Daddy David, but she would have resented it if he had been. He was a calm, quiet person who did not force himself on her, but let her take her own time in getting to know him. He played the piano beautifully and Sanny was in awe of him. Aunt Bertha would sing sometimes, with a sweet, silvery voice, and listening to them she experienced times of great joy. Uncle Nick, seeing her interest in the piano, had offered to teach her, and that was the beginning of a warm, happy relationship which continued for some years, until he, too, disappeared out of her life.

There were two other children in the family, both boys, one older and one younger than Sanny. Half a year after Sanny arrived, the younger boy was adopted by a family in the same town and he departed. Sanny wanted more details about the permanency of adoption. Why couldn't she be adopted?

Because her mother didn't want to give her up, she was told. Supposedly her mother still nurtured hopes of having Sanny return to her one day, a hope everyone including the social workers knew to be unrealistic and probably not very sincere. Sanny's mother spent her time drinking and drying out in a continuous, depressing cycle. Sanny became obsessed with the idea of being adopted, of having a true, permanent family, preferably the one she was in right now. To think of Aunt Bertha as her official, legal mother was true bliss. To have Uncle Nick, kind, quiet, patient Uncle Nick as her father would be the next best thing to having Daddy David come back to life.

But all hopes and dreams came to an end for Sanny when hopes and dreams came true for Uncle Nick. He received the promotion of his life, the ultimate reward for hard studies and hard work, which required a transfer to another state.

Foster-children didn't move across state lines.

After that Sanny didn't care any more. Let them leave, she thought, what do I care? Once more she was moved to another family. She smiled bravely, made a lot of jokes, laughed a lot. She was thirteen years old and her heart was encased in concrete. Her mother died that year and she didn't care. It was too late now. Nobody would want to adopt her now.

But at thirteen it was impossible not to have any hopes and dreams at all. It was at that time that vague fantasies about her own father began to surface again. Maybe he had left her when she was a baby because he hated her mother, and not because she cried all the time at night. Maybe he was searching for her now. Maybe he had been searching for years. It was, somehow, a comforting thought.

Reveries about his eventual return kept recurring for the next several years. Not for Sanny dreams of a prince on horseback; her fantasies favoured a father in a flashy Ferrari.

After breakfast that morning they hiked to the main road, which was narrow, potholed and dusty. The only available transport was a passenger lorry, an ancient Bedford truck rebuilt with narrow wooden benches in

the open back and a colourful, flowery sign that read
BE CONTENT WITH YOUR LOT.

'I guess I'll try,' groaned Mark, as he hoisted
himself and his duffel bag in the back of the *tro-tro*.
Holding out a hand, he helped Sanny in, and she
plopped next to him on the bench. Fortunately there
was a little breathing space left, but for how long it
was hard to say. Usually people were stuffed in like so
many pickles in a jar.

'I'm sorry the limousine I ordered didn't make it,' she
said mockingly. 'But I find this an interesting way to
travel. I've met some very fascinating people this way.'

He nodded. 'And you've got stories to tell.'

'You're catching on.'

She liked him better all the time. She tried to think
of the other men she'd known and how they would
have reacted in similar situations. To begin with, not
one of them would have set foot in Africa in the first
place, but if for the sake of argument she would
suppose they had, every single one of them would
have steered clear of local transportation, local food,
and probably local people.

She glanced at Mark, who was cushioned com-
fortably against a rotund local lady wrapped in a blue
African print cloth and wearing long dangly earrings,
happily engaged in a conversation with her about the
marketing system. The woman was a market mammy,
Sanny gathered, dealing in medicines and medicinal
potions—chemical, herbal, imported, ju-ju—you name
it, she had it, she told Mark with a loud and infectious
laugh.

He told her he was a teacher, and she went on a long
discourse in colourful English about the importance of
education and how she was sending all her children to
secondary school if she could manage it and how she
wanted her sons to be doctors and lawyers and
engineers. She had four of them, so there were enough

of them to go around the various most desirable professions. For her daughters, of which she had two, she had similar aspirations, her main concern being that they would be independent financially, because young men were not to be trusted and didn't make very good husbands these days. Marriage for her daughters was not high on her list of priorities. She had nothing positive to say about her own husband, who was a good-for-nothing and lazed around all day living off her money.

It was an enlightening conversation. Sanny stored it away in her memory to be revived on paper later that day and filed in her special folder.

The vegetation along the road was green and lush. Women and children were walking by the side carrying babies on their backs and baskets of produce on their heads. Here and there fruits and vegetables were sold by the road—bright red tomatoes, big pineapples, baskets full of mangoes and paw-paws and oranges. There were coconuts and onions and okra and huge brown yams and casava roots.

A Land Rover passed them by. It had an English licence plate and the open back was burglar-proofed. It looked like a jail cell on wheels. Behind the bars Sanny noticed a young woman with long blonde hair reading a newspaper. Luggage was stacked up high on top of the roof and tied securely with ropes. World travellers, these.

'Maybe I should have done that,' she said to Mark, pointing at the Land Rover. 'Got myself a car like that and then I could have slept in it and saved money on hotels and I could have sold it again before I came back home.'

'You wouldn't have met all of these fascinating people travelling that way,' he said with a grin.

'Mmm . . . true.' She eyed him speculatively. 'You don't seem to suffer too much, travelling this way.'

'It makes me feel young again. All this dust flying around is good for the ageing process. It does wonders for your lungs and skin and eyes.' With a heart-stopping crash the *tro-tro* smashed into a pothole and bounced out again, shaking and shuddering. 'Not to speak, of course, of what it does for your muscle tone,' he added levelly.

Sanny hung on to him for dear life. People had been known to be thrown out of contraptions like these. The sign on the lorry said to Be Content With Your Lot, but Sanny was not prepared to push that too far.

'We can probably find a bus in Takoradi,' she said reasonably.

'Or a taxi.'

'All the way to Accra? You're crazy! It's too expensive.'

Mark gave her an exasperated look. 'I'll carry the financial burden of this great extravaganza. All I want from you is a gracious acceptance.'

'I've never been very good in the grace department. I don't like you paying my way. It's against my principles,' she said haughtily.

He closed his eyes for a moment as if praying for patience and fortitude. Then he gave her a long-suffering look. 'I don't know why you have to make an issue out of something so trivial. I don't understand why you have to drag principles into something unworthy of so much thought and consideration. I wish you wouldn't make my life so difficult.'

'I feel so sorry for you, I could cry,' said Sanny sarcastically. 'I don't suppose I need to point out that. . . .'

'No, you don't.'

The lorry stopped, and some of the passengers and their cargo of babies and baskets of produce spilled out on to the road, while others clambered on, squeezing in, while everybody made room by snuggling closer together. Sanny and Mark sat squashed together in companionable intimacy, flanked on either side by impressively rounded market mammies. The medicine lady had departed and had been replaced with another, less talkative colleague.

For a while they shook and shuddered down the road without talking. Sanny tried hard not to pay attention to the fact that her thigh and her whole left side in fact was pressed hard against Mark's. It was really quite an exciting feeling, but a *tro-tro* was not the place to be excited. She looked down on the sleeping baby in the lap of the woman next to her. It was very tiny, probably not more than a month old, and the beautiful little brown face looked healthy and peaceful in sleep. She was wearing a minuscule dress with puffy sleeves and lace around the edges and little knitted bootees in case her feet would get cold in the ninety-degree weather. Sanny smiled at the mother, who smiled shyly back.

'How old is she?' asked Sanny.

'Four weeks.'

'She's very beautiful.'

'Thank you.'

'What is her name?'

'Abena.'

'I like that. It's pretty. Is she your first baby?'

The woman smiled. 'Oh, no. I have two sons. They are with my mother.'

This uninspired conversation went on for a little while longer, until Sanny spotted a teenage boy standing by the side of the road holding some furry creature by the tail, showing it to the passers-by as if offering it for sale.

'What was that?' she asked the woman.

'A grasscutter.'

A grasscutter—whatever that was.

'It's for stew,' the woman explained, seeing Sanny's non-comprehending expression.

Sanny turned to Mark, asking if he had seen the boy with the animal and what a grasscutter was. It belonged to the rodent family, he told her, and was some kind of big bush rat.

'The meat is very sweet,' said the woman, 'but it costs plenty.' She shook her head. 'Meat and fish, they cost *too* much now.'

'Have you ever had it?' Sanny asked Mark.

'I've had everything,' he said levelly. 'It's quite good, too, if I remember correctly. I spent some time with Matt and Jackie a couple of years ago and Matt dragged me along on all his expeditions. In the course of that I probably had every delicacy available on the road.'

'It never fails to amaze me how conditioned we are by our cultural background,' Sanny commented, looking at him thoughtfully. 'We like chicken and rabbit and lamb and duck, but that grasscutter gives us nausea just thinking about it. It's all in the head. It makes me wonder about the value of all the other stuff in my head.'

His eyes were laughing. 'It could be very productive to give that some thought now and then.'

What exactly did he mean by that? He put his arm around her shoulder, making both of them more comfortable but also even more closely pressed together. Sanny had the sudden overwhelming urge to put her hand on his leg, to feel the hard muscled strength of it under her fingers, and without further thought, she did. Mark put his free hand on hers and when she raised her eyes to his, he gave her a deep, smouldering look that made her blood race and her heart double its speed. She saw his mouth curl into a grin then and she didn't know whether to burst out laughing or be angry.

She thought again of the night before and of her brave resolution to keep her innermost feelings out of this relationship, to keep them hidden from him at least, and with a sudden overwhelming clarity she knew it wouldn't be possible. With Mark she could never pretend to play some lighthearted game of love and romance. With him she couldn't use the tactics that had been successful with others.

She didn't want to get hurt ever again. She didn't want anybody ever leaving her again. She wasn't going to love anybody ever again. She wasn't going to love him. She wasn't!

The only problem was that she already did.

It had happened like that too when she had met Peter in school. She had been sixteen and for the past three years she'd done an admirable job of keeping everyone at a distance.

After having been deserted by Aunt Bertha and Uncle Nick she had been too numb to cry. She had felt betrayed and abandoned—left behind like a piece of furniture. That was what she had been all along—a piece of societal flotsam that belonged no place. No one had any use for her or her love. Her entire childhood had been nothing but a series of temporary arrangements requiring nothing but temporary love and attachment. Well, she had no more love to spare. Whenever offered it was ultimately discarded one way or another, and she could bear the pain of loss and rejection no more. She had to protect herself.

So Sanny protected herself by closing her emotions up and giving away nothing of what really went on inside her. She would take care of herself from now on. She would smile at the world and tell everyone she was quite happy, perfectly happy. Nobody need worry about her. All she wanted was for everybody to keep their distance.

At first it had been an effort to be joyful and jocular

all the time. Before entering a room she would stop and collect herself for a moment to plaster on a smile and put sparks in her eyes, like a clown putting on his make-up before going on stage. At times her face would ache with the effort to keep the smile in place.

She would stand in front of the mirror practising cheerful expressions. She felt like a brave heroine in some tragic novel—all alone in the world and unloved, but determined to smile till the bitter end and reveal to no one the secret sadness in her soul.

But examining herself in the mirror she had to admit that she didn't look terribly brave or tragic. She looked like a very ordinary teenager, maybe a bit on the short side, but definitely not tragic. Of course, truly tragic heroines belonged in other centuries. They lived in draughty towers in spooky Scottish castles and wore long flouncy skirts. Sanny lived in a snug split level and wore jeans and sneakers.

After a while the laughing and the joking became an unconscious habit, second nature. She memorised jokes—sick jokes, elephant jokes, ethnic jokes—an entire arsenal of jokes for every occasion, for every situation. They were like a weapon or a shield. Nothing better than a joke to ward off unwanted questions or re-route conversations.

Everybody thought she had a terrific personality. She was voted the most popular girl of her class. Sanny was wonderful. Sanny was great fun. Sanny had it all.

Aunt Pat, aunt number four, was no dummy and saw through the masquerade before it was well under way, but she was powerless to do anything about it. Nothing could move Sanny to get close to anybody ever again. Aunt Pat kept trying, but Sanny remained beyond reach, her heart and soul off-limits to all and everybody. Invisible signs were erected all around her like an army—KEEP OUT, NO ACCESS, NO

TRESPASSING. Anybody coming close to forbidden territory was waylaid by some joke about the President's pyjamas or something similarly distracting.

So Sanny protected herself with her army of jokes and her cheerful smiles, her heart a tomb of dead and rejected love, her soul inaccessible.

Until she met Peter.

'Tell me why you're wearing a watch that doesn't work.' Mark's hand moved up to her wrist, covering the watch, and Sanny snatched her hand away as if she'd burned herself.

Peter had given her the watch for her seventeenth birthday, and the fact that Mark had mentioned the thing just as she was thinking about Peter gave her the creeps. It seemed too much of a coincidence.

She had no idea why she was still wearing the watch. Habit, maybe? Or some perverse kind of sentimentality. Or as another tangible, tortuous reminder of her stupidity—like the tattoo on her thigh.

She looked at Mark and shrugged. 'Habit, I suppose. I feel naked without it. I've had it for a long time.'

'Why don't you have it fixed?'

'I tried. It's beyond repair.' Very symbolic, she thought wryly. I'm beyond repair too. I'll never be like I was then. I can never believe in love again. Oh, Peter, why did you have to disillusion me too, like all the others? Didn't you know that with you I'd given myself one more chance?

Of course he had not known, she said to herself. He was eighteen and immature and starting out his life not knowing anything, like every other eighteen-year-old high school football player. How could she have expected mature commitment, eternal devotion, everlasting love when he didn't know what the hell life was all about?

'Did Peter give this to you?'

She stared at Mark, feeling apprehension creep through her. 'What makes you think that?'

His mouth twitched. 'One plus one equals two.'

'You're so smart,' she said disgustedly, and he laughed.

'And right, too. Tell me about this Peter. I find it fascinating that you still seem to be harbouring deep-seated devotion to some high-school boy-friend from the ancient past.'

She was nurturing no devotion, he was wrong about that. If he showed up tomorrow, she wouldn't give Peter the time of day. She was nurturing the loss of her illusions, maybe.

Peter had been a football player, the captain of the team. One look at his well-exercised torso and all her defences had crumbled into rubble. One look into his brown eyes and she had been lost. She'd fallen in love with him with an almost audible crash.

He had bushy brown hair that had a hard time staying in place, and warm, warm brown eyes. (Ever since the Peter fiasco she had avoided men with warm brown eyes, going instead for cool grey or laughing blue.) Since she was one of the most popular girls in school, it was very appropriate for her to fall in love with one of the school's football heroes. They made a great pair—she small and petite, he tall, broad-shouldered and handsome. Everybody envied them.

He was the first boy she had ever allowed to kiss her. She had not allowed much more, even though he had been eager for further experimentation. One thing that was not going to happen to her was pregnancy at sixteen or seventeen. Her own mother had been eighteen when Sanny was born, and she had no desire to follow in her mother's footsteps and present the world with one more sad Sanny.

But the future had held great promise, looking

positively sweet and pink, like spun sugar. With Peter she was going to have the first real permanent home of her life. To start with they would live in a small apartment off campus, because, of course, they would both go to college and get their degrees and become respectable middle class American citizens with two well-behaved, well-adjusted, intelligent children.

In her mind she had had the apartment all furnished and decorated, everything worked out in detail. Crisp flowered sheets on a big bed; soft, lush towels in decorator colours; simple furniture and lots of bright cushions all over the place. She'd secretly picked out the patterns for dishes and glasses and silverware, although she had known deep down that she would probably have to do with stuff from Woolworth's or K-Mart, but dreaming had been fun. As it turned out, she hadn't even needed the stuff from the five and dime. Peter had married his pregnant cheerleader and Sanny had gone to a different college and lived in a dorm room shared with another girl.

Mark was looking at her expectantly and she decided right then and there she might as well satisfy his curiosity and tell him, which she did, in self-derisory fashion, leaving out all the emotional details of her sufferings. She even made him laugh.

So the time passed quite pleasurably on the outside, but less so on the inside. She knew she would have to leave Mark, emotionally as well as physically, as soon as possible, before history could repeat itself. In two days he'd leave for Nigeria and come hell or high water, she wasn't going to meet up with him again anywhere.

They had lunch by the road, small pieces of highly peppered meat on small sticks, which they washed down with fresh coconut milk. They finished the meal with chunks of pineapple and a banana each, and having sat in the shade of a mango tree for a leisurely half hour, went in search of other transport. They were lucky to catch a bus and it was mid-afternoon when they arrived in Accra.

They took a taxi to the Simmons' house, the same type of rinky-dinky vehicle that was ubiquitous in Monrovia and Abidjan. Accra was a more modest town than the other cities, less Westernised and with a more African atmosphere. Sanny did a good bit of observing as they bumped through the potholed streets. The residential area where the Simmons lived sported small, older houses, some in better shape than others. There were chickens and goats in the street as well as children and stray dogs.

As they climbed out of the taxi, the big black iron gate was opened by a bare-chested man who appeared to be the gardener.

'Do they know we're coming?' Sanny asked, and Mark shrugged in answer.

'I sent them a cable, which they probably didn't get yet, and I tried to call them by phone, but I couldn't get through. There's no direct line from Abidjan to Accra, so they have to route the phone calls through Paris and London.'

'You're kidding me!'

'I'm not kidding you,' he said dryly. 'Come on, this way.' He led her around the house, telling the gardener they could find their own way. 'We'll surprise them.'

Rounding the house, she saw a verandah with cushioned chairs, but no people. On the table were two empty glasses and a paperback novel. The big glass doors to the house were left open to catch the breeze, screens closed.

'Anybody home?' Mark called out loud, staying near the screen door without opening it. He grinned at Sanny.

'Just a minute!' A female voice came from

somewhere in the house, and a few moments later there were the sounds of footsteps and then a gasp of delight.

'Mark! I can't believe it!' The door opened and out waddled a small blonde, hugely pregnant.

'Jackie . . . my God, what did you do to yourself!' He moved forward, giving her a hug.

Her laughter was infectious. 'I didn't do it alone, you know!' Big, baby-blue eyes settled on Sanny, and Mark put a possessive arm around Sanny's shoulders and introduced them to each other.

Jackie wasn't more than an inch taller than Sanny, but in everything else the total opposite. She had long blonde hair tucked up on top of her head with numerous little curls escaping around her face. She looked very young and the enormous belly on the tiny frame looked quite preposterous. Blue eyes were full of humour as they looked at Sanny.

'Grotesque, aren't I? It's a miracle I can still move.' She waved at the chairs on the porch. 'Please, sit down and I'll get you something to drink. How about iced tea?' She reached for the two empty glasses on the table. 'Sorry Matt isn't here right now, but he's playing tennis at Tesano. He should be back by six. He's going to be so happy to see you!'

She was bubbling over with enthusiasm, Sanny could tell. 'Let me help you,' she offered, following her globular little figure into the kitchen.

'You're staying here, aren't you?' said Jackie as she took a pitcher of iced tea from the refrigerator. 'The only problem is you'll have to make your own beds because it's our steward's day off and I don't bend over too well anymore.' She grinned cheerfully.

'When's the baby due?' Last month, probably. She looked about ten months pregnant.

'In three weeks.' Jackie groaned. 'I don't know if I'll make it. I told the doctor somebody had made a mistake somewhere in the calculations, but he said no, I just look like a rhino because I carry it all out front and I'm so small.' She let out a suffering sigh. 'You know, I had visions of myself as being very gracefully pregnant. I was going to look regal and serene and beautiful, etcetera, etcetera. I started out having morning sickness, which didn't make me feel very gracious, I can assure you. I looked nicely pregnant for about three days, then I ballooned out with a vengeance. I started huffing and puffing, and serene and beautiful went right out the window.' She plopped several ice cubes into the various glasses and put them on a tray with sugar and lemon slices.

'I'll take it,' said Sanny, picking up the tray.

'I'm sorry,' apologised Jackie, 'if I bore you. I keep talking about myself these days—my body, my baby. It's like an obsession.'

Sanny grinned. 'That's not hard to understand. That baby has obviously taken you over body and soul.'

The heat was oppressive, but there was a soft breeze blowing across the shady porch, stirring the sultry air. The iced tea tasted wonderfully refreshing, especially with the lemon in it. Sanny drank it thirstily as she listened to Mark and Jackie talking, saying very little herself. She didn't know why she felt suddenly totally depressed. Maybe she did know. Her eyes caught some movement and a small lizard, powder blue and orange, slithered past her feet at dizzying speed, startling her for a moment. It went flying off the end of the porch on to the gravel of the driveway.

It was a lovely place, she thought, looking around the yard. Palms swayed royally in the breeze, bougainvillea bushes dripped pink and purple blossoms, banana plants rustled restlessly in untidy clumps.

'Let me show you the accommodation,' said Jackie after a while. She reached a hand towards Mark. 'Help

me up, will you, or I'll never get out of this chair. My
balance isn't what it used to be.'

The guest flat was a cosy little place, bright and
colourful with African print cotton curtains and light
furniture. It had a small verandah of its own, enclosed
with blooming bougainvillea and bright red hibiscus.
Some easy chairs and some potted plants made it a
nice place to sit. There was a sitting room, a bathroom
and a bedroom with a big double bed.

'This was my place when I first came to Ghana a
few years ago,' Jackie commented. 'Now we use it for
guests. We have another spare bedroom in the main
part of the house, if you need it. Come on, I'll show
you.'

If you need it. It was said very casually, very
smoothly. If they wanted to share the guest flat, it was
fine with Jackie. The message was clear. Now was the
time to say something, before Jackie would show them
the other room.

Sanny said nothing, walking out of the flat behind
Jackie without looking at Mark, praying he would
keep silent. He did, but she could feel his eyes on her
back, feel the vibrations as they filed out the door.

It was a small room with a single bed, a chair and a
chest of drawers and an air-conditioning unit in the
wall.

'Take your pick,' said Jackie. 'I'll get the sheets.'
She left the room.

Sanny felt Mark's arm around her shoulder as he
turned her towards him and looked into her face. His
eyes held hers.

'You know, it's quite all right for us to share the
guest flat.'

Her throat was dry and misery like grey fog
surrounded her, filled her. 'It isn't necessary,' she said
calmly, forcing a smile. 'You can have it. I'll take this
room.'

There was a painful, throbbing silence. 'Why?' he said in a low voice, his eyes without laughter.

She shrugged lightly, plastering on the smile, looking bright. 'Why not?' she asked breezily. 'This is a nice little room, don't you think so? It even has air-conditioning. It'll be great. I'll sleep like a baby tonight.'

She stopped talking, noticing suddenly how her legs were trembling. The silence was suffocating. She looked at Mark. She'd never before seen him angry.

And he was angry now.

CHAPTER SIX

His features were hard as granite. Faint fear fluttered through her, but she kept the smile in place.

'Stop jabbering and answer my question,' he said coldly.

Sanny feigned a hurt expression. 'Are you mad at me?'

His fingers hurt her shoulders and anger leaped in his eyes. 'Stop it, Sanny,' he said in a soft, menacing voice. 'Stop the funny business. Why don't you want to share the flat with me?'

She tore herself free and took a step backward. If he wanted her mad, he could have her mad. 'Why should I? You have no right to expect that of me. Just because last night. . . .' Her eyes caught movement at the door, and Jackie came in carrying a bundle of sheets pressed against her chest and resting on her bulging belly. Sanny hurried forward to take them from her, relief flooding through her. 'Here, let me take them.'

They sorted out the sheets and Mark departed to the flat with his, while Sanny stayed behind and began to make up the narrow bed. Jackie lowered herself carefully and slowly on to the chair and Sanny threw her a smiling glance, noticing in that fleeting moment of eye contact Jackie's thoughtful expression. She must have noticed something was wrong. Sanny groaned inwardly as she tucked in the sheet—a pretty print of bright spring flowers, the kind of sheets she'd once dreamed of having on a big marital bed shared with Peter the football player.

Matt was very tall and tanned and sporty-looking in

his white shorts and shirt. He had brown hair curling around his ears and warm brown eyes. He had a lopsided grin and a face that seemed somewhat haphazardly put together, but very masculine and attractive. It was easy to see why Jackie was crazy about him.

In love they certainly were. It radiated from them. Matt had been pleasantly surprised to find them when he came home and had greeted them warmly and enthusiastically. After that he had gone over to Jackie and leaned over to kiss her, and Sanny had noticed how Jackie had grasped his hand and squeezed it. There were other things, little things—the way he looked at her across the table while they were eating their dinner of cold fried chicken and salad, the little teasing remarks, the way he helped her sit down and get up.

They had been married for three years, Jackie had told her. Sanny thought of Laurie who had been married to her Swedish engineer for one and was desperately miserable. Sometimes it worked and sometimes it didn't. Or maybe some people had more sense than others, or a greater capacity for loving, or more tolerance and patience, or more luck.

Whatever it was, she had no more courage to hope for herself. She had learned the hard way that she was better off without dreams and illusions in the love department. So why then did she feel this wave of envy when she looked at Jackie and Matt? Why did they have what she couldn't? What was so special about Jackie that she had all this love and happiness?

She felt mean and uncharitable thinking in those terms, but she couldn't help herself. She was jealous and miserable, and she had avoided looking at Mark practically all evening. Just seeing his face sent sparkles of pain through her. She wasn't going to love him—she couldn't afford to. If she could only manage to live through this weekend she'd be all right.

She went to bed early, claiming fatigue, which was even true. Her body felt ready for collapse and her emotions were worn to a frazzle. She kicked off her sandals, stripped off her dress, and there was a knock on the door.

'Just a minute!' she yelled. Oh, heavens, now what? She didn't have a robe. 'Who is it?'

'Mark,' came the curt reply.

Sanny grabbed the dress and pulled it back over her head, then opened the door, ready to dismiss him. He was inside the room before a sound had come out of her mouth.

'I want a word with you. And don't tell me you're tired and you want to go to bed, because this won't take but a minute.' He sounded in control of himself. His face was expressionless.

She stared at him without responding. Let him say his piece and then get out of her room.

He came a few steps closer and Sanny backed away from him, but he kept coming and she ended up against the wall with him right in front of her.

'Look at me,' he said quietly.

Obediently she lifted her face to his, settling her eyes on a spot between his eyes.

'I want to know what's wrong.'

'Nothing is wrong.' She managed a smile. 'I don't know what you mean.'

'Sanny, don't make me angry!' Mark snapped. 'At some point today something happened, and I have no idea what. Suddenly you're giving me the silent treatment. Suddenly you act as if I'm invisible. I want to know why.' His tone was calm but intense.

She licked dry lips. No way was she going to be able to send him off with some crack or change the subject with some diversionary tactic.

'All right,' she said, looking straight at him. 'I decided that . . .' she swallowed, feeling her voice wobble, '. . . that I've let things go too far. I'm sorry, I didn't mean to be unfair to you.'

'I don't understand. Are you sorry about last night?'

She hesitated for a moment. 'Yes and no. I wish it hadn't happened, but I asked for it myself. And no, because it was . . . good.' Some understatement.

'Well,' he said coolly, 'I'm glad you're not denying that. I won't ask you for the reason of your change of heart, because I have a feeling I'm not going to get a straight answer.'

'It has nothing to do with you.'

'Well, that's a relief,' he commented sarcastically and his tone sent shivers down her spine. Oh, why did it have to come to this?

'I don't suppose either that it would be any use to ask you to come to Nigeria with me.' He reached in his back pocket, pulled something out and handed it to her. She took it from him.

It was an airline ticket in a blue folder. She stared at it, non-comprehending. 'You bought this for me? When?'

'In Abidjan.'

'You didn't tell me.'

'I knew better. The time wasn't exactly ripe.'

For a moment she stared at the ticket in her hand, then held it out to him. 'I'm sorry, but I can't accept,' she said evenly.

'Keep it. Do with it what you like.' His voice was hard. He turned and strode out of the room.

Her jaws clenched hard, she tore the ticket cold-bloodedly in half and dropped the pieces into the waste basket. So that was that. She felt dead inside, but she was familiar with the sensation. She could handle it; she was very accomplished at handling dead feelings.

'You're coming to Nigeria with me whether you like it or not,' Mark said to her in her dream. 'You're coming on the damn plane with me if I have to drag you on there bodily. You think you can do as you please and have no consideration for my feelings, but I'll teach you differently! I didn't spend so much time on you for nothing, coming to Accra with you, sitting on those damned decrepit lorries for the hell of it. I want you with me. I want you in my bed. You're staying with me from now on until I tell you you can leave, and not until I'm good and ready. Not until I've had enough of you, until I don't want you any more.'

His words flooded over her without mercy and she couldn't talk. Her jaws wouldn't move. Her mouth was rigid, her lips like rubber. Her tongue ... she couldn't even feel her tongue. Terror gripped her. What had happened to her tongue? She couldn't move, either, because he held her prisoner against the wall, pressing against her so she couldn't escape.

'We'll go back to the States and you'll live with me and you can write your book in my study while I'm lecturing. And every day when I come home we'll make love. We'll make love all night long and you'll not want to go away. You'll stay with me until I say you can leave. You'll stay until I throw you out.'

He had a beautiful old house with expensive furniture and lots of Oriental carpets and wood carvings from all over the world. For years on end, Sanny wandered through the house, from room to room. She never said a word—not to Mark, not to anyone. She could no longer speak. So she stayed with him and slept with him in the big bed with the pretty flowered sheets, and she took long hot showers and dried herself on thick soft towels in luscious colours, and they drank champagne every night after making love.

'You see?' he said triumphantly. 'I can make you

happy.' And she smiled and nodded, not speaking, not feeling anything. She was not happy. She was not unhappy, either. She felt vacant, as if she were only a shell, an empty body with an empty mind.

Her father came to the house one day. He was tall and handsome with silver-grey hair and a healthy tan. He drove a white Ferrari with red leather upholstery. He told her how much he had always loved her and how long it had taken him to finally find her. He had spent thousands of dollars and endless hours on his search. Long sleepless nights he had worried about her, poor darling. There were tears in his eyes as he put his arms around her and hugged her. He smelled like vanilla. From now on, he said, everything would be all right because they were finally together. His wife at home was waiting anxiously to meet her because she had always wanted a daughter and now she had one. They had a room ready for her, full of beautiful, expensive toys.

Suddenly there was a big party and everybody was having a wonderful time drinking palm wine and eating roasted plantain and peppery meat on little sticks. The party was in Sanny's honour, to celebrate the phenomenal success of her book. She was famous now, just like everybody else present. Robert Redford was there, and Billy Graham and Woody Allen and Jane Fonda in leotards, doing sit-ups. Frank Sinatra was crooning schmaltzy love songs and Carol Burnett was dancing in a can-can outfit.

David Frost and Johnny Carson were having a fight about who was going to interview her first, which was very amusing since she couldn't talk. Nobody at the party seemed to have noticed. David began to insult Johnny because his show was a flop in England and nobody there understood him and his bizarre humour. Johnny said nobody in America understood David because he spoke as if he had a hot potato in his throat.

It was a lovely party.

Everybody told her how wonderful her book was and how interesting and fascinating it was to read all about rubber plantations and coconut oil extraction plants and about the lady selling ju-ju medicine. The President, who was present too, made a special point of saying how important it was to learn more about the world around us. Understanding each other was the first step to peace, he explained. He was looking forward to throwing all the nuclear weapons in the ocean, right along with the surplus cheese and chickens (it was too expensive and too complicated to send the stuff to starving nations, he clarified). Sanny nodded silently and smiled serenely because she still couldn't talk.

And then she saw Mark coming through the door with a sleek slinky blonde hanging on his arm, and somebody said she was a cheerleader and he was going to marry her because she was pregnant and was going to have twins. They glided towards her, as if in church already, and Mark smiled warmly at her.

'You can leave now,' he said. 'I don't need you any more—I've got her. Here's a ticket to Nigeria.'

And then Sanny picked up a wood carving of some African fertility queen and hit him over the head with it, and he collapsed on the floor right at her feet.

She was sitting up in bed, sweating and shivering, her heart beating painfully in her chest. There was a knock on the door and someone came in, but she wasn't sure who. It was very dark.

'Are you all right?' A light came on and she blinked uncomfortably.

He was very tall, with brown hair and warm brown eyes that looked at her with great concern. He was wearing a short terry cloth bathrobe, his hands pushed into the pockets. It was Matt Simmons.

'I guess I was dreaming,' Sanny explained.

'And screaming,' he added dryly.

'Screaming?' She couldn't believe it. She didn't remember that. She wiped the hair off her forehead. Her skin was clammy.

'You screamed "I killed him! I killed him!" over and over again. Jackie heard you; she doesn't sleep very well these days. She woke me up.' Matt looked at her searchingly.

'Oh . . . I'm terribly sorry! I didn't realise I was making so much noise.' She took a deep breath. 'I was dreaming about cockroaches—those huge ones. I was trying to kill them.' She shuddered. 'It was awful!'

'It must have been.' There was a flicker of amusement in the brown eyes. 'Would you like something cold to drink?'

'Oh, no, please don't bother. I'm all right.'

'It's no bother. Water? Juice?'

She hesitated. 'Do you have any milk?'

'Only the powdered variety.'

'Of course. I'd like some of that. But I can get it myself.'

'You stay right there. I'll be back in a minute.'

Sanny lay back on the pillow, feeling drained and exhausted. Well, she had the right to be. She'd lived through a lot in the last few hours—a full-fledged affair with Mark, a meeting with the President who'd wanted to throw all the nuclear weapons in the ocean, a murder. Her dreams were getting positively bizarre!

Matt came back in with a glass of milk and handed it to her. 'Guess who else is up,' he remarked.

'Who?' She drank thirstily from the cold milk.

'Mark. He's sitting out on the verandah feeding himself to the mosquitoes. I saw him through the window.'

'He couldn't have heard me all the way over there.'

'No. He probably had a bad dream too—cockroaches or something.'

'Or something.' She handed him the glass, determined not to get drawn into conversation. 'Thank you very much. I'm sorry I woke you and Jackie up—really.'

'Don't worry about it. Hope you sleep well. Goodnight.'

'Goodnight.'

Like hell, she thought. She was wide awake. She saw herself standing over Mark sprawled on the floor, a wood carving in her hand. She began to shake and then, slowly and silently, tears began to stream down her face.

Sunday was a nightmare, a smiling, joking, nightmare. Battling dark depression, Sanny tried to appear cheerful and sizzling with vitality. All she wanted to do was hide in some dungeon and never see Mark again. The friction between them jangled her nerves, but she covered it up with spirited talk and sprightly smiles. She tried to ignore the hard set of his jaw that seemed to get harder and more rigid by the hour, tried not to notice the cold bleakness in his eyes. Now and then, as she made some crack or joke, she saw the anger flare up in his eyes and she avoided looking at him as much as possible.

Matt and Jackie acted as if they noticed nothing, but Sanny knew they were well aware of the sparks flying left and right. She felt ungracious and rude. I've got to leave here, she thought. I can't stay in the house of strangers under these circumstances. Tomorrow I'll find myself a hotel.

She tried to avoid being alone with Mark, but in the evening after dinner they happened to be alone for a few unfortunate moments.

'You're giving quite a performance,' he remarked coolly. 'You amaze me.'

'I don't know what you're talking about,' she said airily. 'Your friends are nice. Jackie isn't what she looks, is she?'

He ignored that. 'You're nice too,' he said sarcastically. 'Like soda water. All bubbles and no taste.'

She fought off the hurt of the insult, shrugging nonchalantly. 'I see no reason for you to be so offensive. Did I wound your precious male ego by not wanting to share your bed? Am I supposed to be your willing slave once you've demonstrated your talents? I. . . .'

Oh, God, what am I doing? What am I saying? She saw his face grow pale under his tan. His eyes were like glacial ice.

'My God,' he said in a low voice, 'you're a phoney!' He came to his feet and marched out the room as if he could stand the sight of her no longer.

Sanny was shaking all over. She pressed her palms against her closed eyes, trying hard to calm her shattered nerves. How could she have said such a vile, mean thing? She didn't recognise herself any more. Another part of her was emerging, something with claws and horns and a barbed-wire tongue.

'Where's Mark?'

She raised her head and found Jackie looking at her, a tray with cups of coffee in her hands. She swallowed.

'I don't know. He just left a moment ago. Let me take this.' She jumped out of the chair, reached for the tray and put it on the table.

Jackie observed her with a frown. 'Are you all right?'

'I'm fine,' Sanny said evenly, avoiding Jackie's eyes and sitting back down. I wish I were dead, she thought.

Matt, too, returned to the room, sat down and took his coffee from the table and began to recount a story about some local ceremony he had attended the previous week. It had involved a brass band, a sound truck, a long procession with drummers, chiefs carried around in coloured palanquins, and a fetish priestess dressed in white with chalk on her face and arms.

It would have been a great event for her to have witnessed, he said. It would have been good material. Yes, she said, it would have been. She was sorry, she said. Maybe she'd be lucky some other time. He smiled. She smiled. Jackie smiled. Mark came back in the room, unsmiling, sat down and drank his coffee in silence.

Sanny excused herself as soon as she could, went back to her room, took a long cool shower, doused herself with Jungle Jasmin talcum powder and went to bed with an Agatha Christie novel.

In the middle of the night she awoke, shivering and icy cold. She'd forgotten to turn down the air-conditioner and it was going full blast. She'd fallen asleep reading, without even a sheet covering her. She turned the machine off and opened the window, feeling the steamy, sultry night air flowing past her into the room. It felt soothing on her cold skin. Freezing to death in the tropics, she thought wryly, just the thing to happen to me!

She stood in front of the window looking out into the shadowy darkness, hearing the vibrating screeching of masses of crickets in the grass. A full moon peeped through the fronds of the coconut palm in the neighbours' compound.

A sound caught her attention—not the whispering of leaves or some other night sound. Footsteps. Slow, soft. Her mouth went dry. Don't be ridiculous, she thought, it's the night watchman, of course. Ali, just

Ali. But she couldn't see anything, only hear the slow, careful steps of somebody's feet. Then suddenly a figure came into sight—a long, ghostly white robe eerily illuminated by the moonlight, and above it a head covered in some sort of polar hat that left only eyes and mouth exposed. Her heart leaped in her throat. This was not Ali! The man held a stick, thick like a club, in one hand and was slowly approaching her window.

Her heart pounding, Sanny let the curtains drop back and sat down on the bed.

If she'd ever seen anyone who looked as if he had evil intentions, this one was it. He looked like something out of a movie. She heard him move past the window. Who was he? Back at the window, she peered into the dark and saw a second spooky apparition—another man in a long white Muslim robe. This one only had a cap on his head and no club in his hand, but she had not seen him around and it wasn't Ali. There were soft whispering voices and then she saw the hooded man retrace his steps and meet the other. They stood talking quietly for some minutes while Sanny's panic grew.

She'd have to do something. These characters were robbers, most likely. Where was Ali? Had he fallen asleep? The men were going to come in if she didn't do something. They would steal the Simmons' new small stereo they'd brought back from the States on their last leave. They would take Jackie's sewing machine, the iron, the powdered milk, the flour, the sugar, the cooking oil.

Don't sit there, you idiot, do something! Wake somebody up!

What if she was wrong? What if these two spooky characters were perfectly legitimate? But how? Where was Ali? Her legs were quivering as she crossed to the door. She didn't want to pound on Matt and Jackie's door. She felt funny about waking them up, she had no idea why. She trotted through the hall, into the living room to the connecting door to the guest flat. The door was not locked, and quietly she entered the flat. The bedroom door was closed and she could hear the monotonous hum of the air-conditioner at work. She knocked on the door. 'Mark! Wake up!' she called.

No sound, no movement. She knocked and called again, and waited. Nothing. She opened the door slightly and looked inside. Moonlight streaked across the bed through an opening in the curtains. Mark's sleeping body lay stretched out under the sheet, his shoulders bare. He had to be out cold not to have heard her calling.

Heart racing, Sanny stood in the door and watched him. Two nights earlier she'd been in bed with him, his arms around her, close, so close. Staring at his shadowed face, she felt again the warm muscled body against her, felt again his hands touching her body, his mouth on hers. In one fleeting moment she remembered everything, lived through it once more. A tremor ran through her and she was no longer cold. In one treacherous moment of weakness she was prepared to throw all sanity overboard, forget her fear, forget about tomorrow and the pain it would bring.

She took a deep breath and advanced into the room, remembering the men outside. 'Mark! Wake up!'

He stirred, muttering something sleepily. She called again and then he sat up, the sheet falling away from his chest. He raked a hand through tousled hair and stared at her.

'Sanny?' He sounded as if he wasn't sure he was seeing right.

'Mark, there are two men outside,' she said urgently. 'They look suspicious—I'm afraid they might try to break in.'

'Men? Where's Ali?'

'I didn't see him! One of these guys has his face all covered up and he's carrying a stick and. . . .'

He leaped out of bed with a surge of energy and began to pull on his jeans. Sanny turned and walked back into the living room.

What you don't need now, she told herself miserably, is to see him naked and gorgeous. Why didn't he wear baggy grandpa pyjamas?—striped, blue and grey, shapeless, with a little breast pocket and a tie-string around the waist. Everything decently tied and buttoned up. No, not Mark. He had jumped out of bed without a stitch on.

'Where are they?' He was behind her and she turned around.

'They were out in front of my window in the back yard.'

'Let's see.' He strode through the connecting door into the living room.

In her bedroom he opened the curtain and peered into the dark. 'I see them,' he said softly. 'That one guy in the mobster get-up is Ali. I don't know who the other one is. I'll check it out.'

Be careful, she wanted to say, but he was gone already. She sank down on the bed, feeling like a complete fool. There was probably nothing the matter. The two men had been talking amicably enough, and if one of them was Ali then the other probably was equally innocent. But why would Ali dress up like something out of a gangster movie?

She got up and padded quietly to the kitchen, finding the door slightly open. Mark came in a moment later and locked it carefully behind him.

'The other man is the *night watch* from across the street. They're just having a little nocturnal chat. Everything is hunky-dory.'

Sanny expelled a deep sigh. 'Well, leave it to me to dream up great tragedies for no reason at all! I had them stealing the stereo and the sewing machine and the sugar.'

'I don't blame you,' he said. 'Ali looks a sight with that hat pulled over his face.' Mark's face was expressionless, his voice toneless.

Sanny folded her arms in front of her breasts, feeling awkward. She stared at his bare chest and the rough curly hair covering it.

'Why is he decked out like that?' she asked. 'And how did you know it was him?'

'I saw him last night before I went to bed. He says he does it to scare off the *teefs*. It probably works as long as he doesn't fall asleep in his chair.' He moved suddenly, taking a glass out of a cabinet and reaching for a bottle of Scotch. 'Would you like a drink? You look like you need one.'

'No, thanks—I'd like some milk, though. I suppose it's all right if I just help myself?'

'If I were you I wouldn't wake them up just to ask, I'm quite sure you're very welcome to a glass of milk.'

Sanny clenched her jaws. He was mocking her, and it made her mad. 'They may be *your* close friends, but they aren't mine. I'm not in the habit of prowling around people's houses raiding refrigerators and kitchen cabinets and helping myself to whatever I want.'

He leaned lazily against the counter and let his eyes rove over her in derisory fashion. 'Why don't we make an issue out of it?' he suggested sardonically. 'We can have an all-out fight about a lousy glass of powdered milk, instead of about whatever it is that's really bugging you.'

She suppressed an angry reply and turned her back on him, opening the refrigerator. 'I don't fight in the middle of the night. And I'm peachy keen; nothing's bugging me. You're the one who seems to be bothered.' She took the pitcher of milk out and closed the refrigerator door. Fingers closed around her wrist in a painful grip and the pitcher of milk was taken out of her suddenly lifeless fingers and deposited on the counter. Mark twisted her around so she was facing him and he clamped his hands around her upper arms, holding her in place.

She saw the anger in his eyes and her throat went dry. Her heart fluttered nervously. Now look what you've done, said her Other Self. You've made the tiger mad. You should know better than that.

His eyes hypnotised her and she couldn't look away to save her life.

'Sanny,' he began in a cool, low voice, 'one night I'm holding a warm, willing woman in my arms, and the next she won't even talk to me. Am I not supposed to be bothered by that? What kind of a man do you think I am? I'm not into the one-night-stand routine—I've found that very unsatisfactory in the past. I didn't come along with you to Accra just for a little nocturnal bliss.'

'You're lucky, you got it anyway. What the hell are you complaining about?' Her legs were trembling. She was losing her sanity, saying all the wrong things.

His face grew taut. 'Stop it, Sanny! You can't blame me for taking what was given to me freely. I didn't force you and I didn't seduce you, so for God's sake don't play the outraged innocent!'

A laugh escaped her, an hysterical little laugh that almost brought tears to her eyes. 'You've got it all wrong! I'm not blaming you for anything at all. I'm only telling you that I don't want to sleep with you any more, and that I don't want to come along with you to Nigeria and that I don't want you to follow me around any more.'

'I'm not asking you to sleep with me,' he said in a tightly controlled voice. 'I'm asking you to talk to me. *Talk* to me, Sanny.'

'No,' she said tonelessly. 'There's nothing to say. Please let me go.'

He didn't. He looked at her with dark eyes and the silence stretched her nerves to breaking point. 'I can't,' he said then, and the odd, husky note in his voice surprised her. With a groan he pulled her to him, kissing her with a wild, impatient fierceness that shocked her into motionless surrender.

For the past two days she had carefully suppressed her emotions and yearnings, put them in cold storage and covered them up with laughter and jokes. She was expert at that tactic, but why did it not work now? Why was it so easy for him to break through all her defences? Why couldn't she keep a cool front? *Come on, tiger, let go of me. This is the kitchen in somebody else's house. Cool it.* It's what she would have said to any other man intent on seduction without her co-operation. She would have laughed and made some wisecrack. But she was incapable of it now.

She felt his lips on hers, hard and demanding, his body pressed close against hers, and she had no will and no power to fight him off. Something outside herself, some force she had no control over, took hold of her mind and thoughts and body. She responded to Mark's kisses with a hunger and a desperation so intense it trembled through her limbs. Her whole body was aglow, full of a feverish sensation that swirled through her blood.

His hands moved over her body, her bare skin—her nightgown lay in a heap around her feet—as images of remembered loving whirled through her head and the longing was like a pain. She moaned, and he murmured something, but she didn't hear quite what. Maybe *I love you, Sanny.*

I love you, Sanny. Her mind echoed the imagined words, producing images and sensations, almost real, of smiling eyes and tender touches and sweet words of love.

I love you, Sanny.

I love you, Mark. For ever and ever and ever.

Light and laughter and elation. Warmth and euphoria and happiness for ever.

Not for ever. There is no for ever, Sanny.

This time it's different. This time. . . .

I can only stay a little while. Goodbye, Sanny, I have to leave.

Goodbye, Sanny. . . . With the strength of panic, she tore herself away. She reached behind her and grasped the counter for support, seeing sudden dark astonishment in his eyes.

'Sanny. . . .'

'Keep away from me!' Her voice was an agonised squeak. 'I'm not going to let it happen to me again, not ever, ever again! I'd rather *die*! You're not going to get the chance to do it to me like all the others, because I won't let it happen! I won't let it happen, you hear? So you keep your hands off me! You leave me alone! I don't want you, you understand. I *don't want you*! I. . . .' Her voice broke in a sob. Bending over, she lifted up her nightgown and slid the straps back over her shoulders.

In a flash of movement Mark had taken hold of her arms again and shook her. 'You calm down,' he ordered in a tight voice. 'And you explain yourself.'

'You let me go, or I'll scream! I'll scream and wake everybody up!' She tried to wrench herself free, but it was no use.

He shook her again. 'Sanny, you're hysterical! If you don't take control of yourself I'll slap you.'

'Oh, you'd like that, wouldn't you?' she spat. 'Get your paws off me, or so help me God, I'll scream!' She kicked him on the shin, but it was a pathetic gesture, since she had only a bare foot to work with. Next thing she knew he had swung her up into his arms and clamped one hand over her mouth. He carried her out of the kitchen and across the living room to the connecting door to the guest flat.

Her kicking and squirming had no effect whatsoever and she was dumped on his bed without ceremony. He held her down with his legs and arms and looked at her with eyes that were cold and angry, and fear choked her.

There was a moment of vibrating silence.

'Now,' he said then, 'first things first.'

CHAPTER SEVEN

SANNY closed her eyes as cold anger ran through her. 'I won't forgive you,' she whispered fiercely. 'I'll never, *never* forgive you! Remember that!'

Mark gave a low laugh that held no amusement. 'Rape isn't my style, Sanny. I like my loving in a more amicable atmosphere. There hasn't been a time yet that I've felt less like making love than I do now.'

'Then get off me! I hate you! I hate what you're doing to me!' To her horror another sob broke loose.

'What am I doing to you?' His tone was cool.

'You're holding me down! You carried me over here, dumped me like so much garbage! You're manhandling me and I hate you! Nobody treats me like this! *Nobody*, you hear?'

His expression didn't change. 'I don't like being rough, but you left me no choice,' he said calmly.

'Oh, listen to this! Mr Cool and Composed Takes Control! Well, you can forget it, Professor. Nobody takes control of me except me! So let me go! Take your hands off me!' She struggled wildly against him, feeling her senses leave her in an uncontrollable rage fired by helpless humiliation. It swirled inside her, taking over, consuming her. She didn't know what she was saying any more—words came out on their own volition, a torrent of verbiage she had no power to stop. She struggled fiercely while sentences came pouring out in an unrelenting current of emotion, until suddenly all resistance broke as she felt the stinging pain of a slap on her cheek.

She gasped, then lay still, staring up into his face in silent shock. He looked pale and strained.

'I'm sorry,' he said, his voice oddly anguished. 'I didn't like doing that, but I had to.'

Sanny felt as if she'd woken up out of some horrible nightmare. My God, she thought in horror, I went wild! I lost my senses. I must have been hysterical.

She closed her eyes and covered her face with her hands, feeling the wetness of tears on her cheeks. A moan came from somewhere deep inside her and a tremor ran through her and then she was weeping helplessly. She had no strength to hold it back and she didn't even try.

Mark pulled her closer to him, holding her in his arms without force. 'It's all right,' he said softly. 'Go ahead and cry, it's all right.'

When it was all over she lay against him, spent, feeling only emptiness and cold. She didn't want to feel anything ever again. Disengaging herself from his arms, she sat up. 'I'll go now,' she said tonelessly.

He took her hand. 'Sanny, why don't you tell me about it?'

'No.' She snatched her hand away and got off the bed. 'I'm all right—don't worry.'

'I didn't hit you out of anger. I want you to understand that,' he said.

'I know that. I went crazy. I understand perfectly.' She walked to the door on trembling legs. 'Goodnight.'

He was behind her, not touching. 'Sanny, please,' he said quietly, 'don't go like this. We have to talk.'

'I don't want to talk. There's nothing I can say that will do us any good, believe me.' Her eyes met his for a painful moment, then, head bent, she opened the door and went out. Mark didn't follow.

She'd seen the bleakness in his eyes, seen the iron control of his body and in a flash of insight she realised what it had cost him to let her go.

In the kitchen she poured herself some milk and leaned against the counter to drink it.

I don't care, she thought. I don't care what he feels or thinks. All I care about is myself—I've got to take care of myself. In the final analysis nobody ever cared about me and my feelings. In the end he'd leave me like everybody else, and I can't take that any more. I can't afford to let it happen again.

She took a deep breath, feeling an increasing sense of determination settle inside her. I'm going to be all right, she thought. I'm going to be all right.

Drinking the last of the milk, she heard soft movement and her eyes caught sight of Jackie in a long, tent-like nightgown padding across the living room towards the kitchen. She grinned when she saw Sanny.

'Couldn't you sleep either? I keep thinking I'm the only one awake in the world. I'm up half the night nowadays. Junior keeps kicking me and I can't get comfortable any more. It's awful.' She opened the refrigerator and peered inside, sighing heavily. 'I supposed I should have some of this miserable milk. If I didn't have to I'd never touch the stuff.' Her eyes settled on the glass in Sanny's hand. 'Don't tell me you're drinking it voluntarily!'

'At home I drink milk all the time,' Sanny explained. 'I couldn't kick the habit.'

'I admire your courage,' Jackie said with a grimace. 'Let's sit in the living room. Gravity is giving me problems these days.' She waddled out of the kitchen and Sanny followed her. She was wide awake, so there was no sense in her going back to bed.

Gravity wasn't Jackie's only problem. It was a veritable balancing act to sit down, and Sanny couldn't help laughing as she watched her.

Jackie glowered at her. 'Don't you laugh,' she said darkly. 'Just you wait! It may be even worse for you—

you're shorter than I am.' She stopped talking and her expression changed. 'You've been crying! What's wrong?'

Sanny grinned cheerfully, relieved to find how easy it was. 'Don't look so stricken. I do it once a week, whether I need it or not.'

Jackie's eyes ran over the rest of her and her face grew pale. 'My God, you look mauled!' Her voice was low and she looked appalled. 'What's been going on here?'

Sanny offered a reassuring look, imagining the atrocities Jackie must be thinking had taken place under her roof. 'Don't jump to conclusions. I've been neither raped nor ravished.' She grimaced. 'All we had was a friendly little midnight skirmish.' Well, maybe it had been more like the Battle of the Bulge.

Jackie was not amused. 'What happened? Mark isn't exactly the violent type. He . . .'

'He wasn't violent.' No more than she had been, anyway. 'I'm all in one piece—no broken bones.'

'Look at your arms!'

Sanny shrugged, unconcerned. 'Just the result of a little passion run amok. Nothing to worry about.'

'By tomorrow they'll win an award in a colour contest!'

'I bruise easily. Lack of vitamin C, they say. You'd think I'd have had enough, though, with all the fruit I've been eating lately—oranges and pineapples. . . . There's C in Pineapple, isn't there?' Sanny smiled brightly.

Jackie didn't. She looked at her closely. 'I don't like this. What got into him? Actually, I guess I know what got into him. You haven't made it easy for him, have you?' Her face changed and she looked remorseful. 'I'm sorry, I didn't mean to sound so sanctimonious. It's none of my business.'

Sanny had no desire to confide in her. She wanted

to forget the whole thing. Jackie was happily married
and blooming with baby—how could she possibly
understand about her feelings and fears? For years
she'd kept them to herself, not letting anyone in on
her innermost self. It was better so.

'It's all right. Actually, I woke him up because I
thought there were two *teefs* outside trying to take off
with your flour and your furniture. They turned out
to be the night watch from across the street and Ali
cooking his head in a knitted snow hat.'

Jackie finally laughed. Relieved, Sanny began to tell
her about the incident.

Mark and Matt were both gone when Sanny woke up
the next morning. Jackie was still at the breakfast
table, sipping tea.

'They'll be gone for the day,' she said. 'Matt had
work to do in the Volta Region and Mark decided to
go along. Did you get some sleep after we went to
bed?'

Sanny sat down at the table. 'Some,' she said
vaguely. She'd been too keyed up to sleep much.
She'd merely dozed for the remainder of the night, not
getting much rest. Fortunately, Mark was gone, so at
least she didn't need her strength to deal with him.
She was beginning to feel better already. It was a relief
she didn't have to face him for some hours yet.
Tomorrow he would leave for Nigeria and she could
start breathing easy again. Everything would be fine.
Life wasn't so bad. Look at the sunshine outside, she
told herself, the flowering frangipani, the bougainvillea, the palms. This is exotic Africa. Things could be a
lot worse. I could have been in downtown Detroit
writing obituaries.

Kwesi, the steward, a man of formidable proportions, came in and served her breakfast of fried eggs
and toast and sliced pineapple and orange juice.

Vitamin C, here you go, she commented silently as she drained the glass. Go to work on my bruises. They weren't all that bad. That, too, could have been worse.

'Do you know where the American Consulate is?' she asked Jackie.

'Sure. Two streets down from here, believe it or not.' She frowned. 'Any problems?'

'Problems? Oh, no. I just like to check in, so to speak, and leave my name, just in case anybody from home needs to contact me. Somebody suggested I shouldn't just disappear in the blue yonder, and I suppose he was right.' Sanny shrugged. 'Not that I can imagine any emergency that would make it necessary for me to go home.'

'What about your family? God forbid, but something could happen.' Jackie poured herself another cup of tea and eyed her somewhat strangely.

'I don't have any family,' she said evenly. How many times she had said that sentence in her life she had no idea.

'Nobody?' Jackie looked amazed. 'No grandparents or aunts and uncles?'

'Nobody I know of.' She chewed a piece of toast and swallowed it. 'My father may still be roaming the face of the earth some place, I don't know. My mother is dead and so are my grandparents. My mother was an only child, so that takes care of that side of the family.' She shrugged 'My father's family I never knew. I never knew him either, for that matter. He left my mother when I was three months old.' She chewed her toast, watching Jackie's expression. 'What about you? You have relatives?'

Jackie nodded. 'I'm lucky. I've both my parents and a brother, and two out of four grandparents and scores of aunts and uncles and cousins. It must have been hard for you as a child, without your father.'

Without my mother too, most of the time, Sanny

added silently. She produced a carefree grin. 'I
managed. You see here in front of you a perfectly
normal, well-adjusted waif. No pity necessary.'

'You didn't strike me as the pitiful type,' Jackie said
dryly, her baby-blue eyes observing her thoughtfully.

'Thank God!'

Somehow she'd managed to finish her food—more
food than she'd eaten for breakfast in months. She
groaned. 'I shouldn't have eaten all that. I won't be
able to move for at least an hour.'

'Count yourself lucky. I haven't been able to move
for months.' Jackie paused. 'By the way, when Mark
leaves tomorrow, you're staying on, aren't you?'

'In Accra, you mean? For a couple of more days,
yes. Then I'm going up north, Upper Volta, Niger. At
least that's what my itinerary says. It's very loose,
though. I have no set plans really. If something
interesting comes up I want to be able to go with it.
Now that we're talking about it,' she added, 'do you
know a decent second-rate hotel? I don't need an air-
conditioner, but the rats I can do without.'

'Why don't you stay here? I'd like that.'

Sanny eyed her doubtfully. Jackie sounded as if she
meant it. For some reason she had had the distinct
feeling that Jackie did not altogether approve of her.
She had shrugged off the feeling, having no desire to
analyse it. Mark was their friend and she was not, and
with the obviously crackling tension between Mark
and herself, it was no wonder that Jackie might feel
suspicious of her.

'Thanks, but no. I don't want to impose on you, and
there's no need, really.'

Jackie insisted. Please, she said, she was bored.
She'd stopped working the week before and didn't
know what to do with herself. She'd like the company.
After two more pleases Sanny accepted. Kwesi
brought in more coffee for her, and they sat around

the table lazily and talked about the heat and the shortages of food and the economic conditions and Sanny's work. Jackie wanted to read some of her writing and Sanny got it for her. Mark had wanted to read her columns too, but he hadn't yet, and never would now. Then, leaving Jackie to it, she went to the Consulate and after that took a taxi into town to look around.

The heat was sweltering, the air steamy, and she was wet and sticky with perspiration almost from the start. Her sunglasses kept sliding down her nose and her eyes ached with the brightness of the sunlight despite the glasses. I must be crazy, she thought, traipsing around in the heat! I hardly slept last night. I might pass out from exhaustion right here in the market with my face in somebody's tomatoes. Go home, have a siesta, and do some typing this afternoon if you can get hold of a typewriter. Tomorrow is another day.

She slept for two hours and dreamed about Mark. He said he loved her and wanted to marry her and would never leave her. All she had to do was believe him. She said that that was the whole problem: she had trouble believing in fairy tales. He said this was no fairy tale. This was true and real, and she should believe him because everybody always believed him. He was a very credible person.

She woke up to the sound of loud laughter leaping up above the hum of the air-conditioner. It was coming from outside, from the direction of the servants' quarters. 'Go ahead,' she muttered morosely, 'laugh, have fun, don't mind me.'

She got out of bed, straightened the sheets, slipped into a clean pink dress and brushed her hair. Her eye caught the bright blue of the torn-up airline ticket on the bottom of the wastebasket.

I could tape it together, she thought.

You will do no such thing, ordered her ever-watchful Other Self. Besides, it's too late. You don't even have a visa for Nigeria.

I can get one tomorrow and go a day later.

Forget it. Mark wouldn't want you any more. Not after all the things you said to him.

I can apologise. I'll tell him. . . .

Don't be stupid! Stop it while you still can! Going to Nigeria will be your downfall!

She stared at herself in the mirror, seeing only a blurred image of herself. Damn, damn! she thought, throwing the hairbrush on the bed with a vicious thrust of her wrist. It bounced off on to the floor. She left it where it fell and swung out of the door.

Jackie was sitting outside on the verandah, a pitcher of lemonade on the table. 'Sit down and join me,' she invited. 'I read your stuff. It surprised me.'

'Oh? How?'

'I guess I was expecting the standard type of travel story—a lot of observation and not too much contemplation. In a lot of those tales the people tend to be treated as part of the scenery, rather than human beings with feelings and thoughts that might be worth knowing and understanding.' She paused for a moment and smiled. 'I like your interviews. The people are very real.'

'They *were* real life individuals when I talked to them, you know,' said Sanny, grinning, feeling more pleased than she wanted to admit to herself.

'You know,' Jackie said, laughing suddenly, 'last time Matt and I were on home leave in the States, some woman asked me, "Do you bump into a lot of natives over there?" and I said, "Natives? Oh, you mean Africans! Yes, as a matter of fact I do bump into a few now and then. Actually I have some living right next door. He's a doctor and his wife is a teacher. And I buy my eggs from one, and my bread, too. And now

that I come to think of it, my dentist is one too. It *is*
their country, you know." She looked at me as if I was
crazy. I was surprised at myself—I don't usually
bestow my sarcasm on to innocent ignorants, but I'd
had a drink and I was fed up about something.' She
grinned unrepentantly. 'I'll never forget her face!'

Sanny grimaced. 'I was shocked by my own
ignorance when I came here. I spent two days in my
hotel room, too scared to come out.'

'What were you afraid of?'

'I'm not really sure. It made me feel very
uncomfortable to be in the minority. I was a stranger
and I didn't belong. Maybe I had a fear of some
people ganging up on me and telling me to get the hell
out of their country.' She grinned. 'When I finally got
brave enough to go out I found everybody so friendly
and hospitable that I felt like a fool. That's when I
started to think of writing my stories in terms of
people—their lives, their work, their feelings.'

'Your book is going to be wonderful, I'm positive,'
Jackie told her. 'I hope you can find a good publisher.'

Ah, praise is so good for the soul, Sanny thought.
She sipped lemonade, letting her eyes travel around
the garden, seeing the bright colours of flowering
things and lush vegetation, and her thoughts went
back, relentlessly, to Mark. I've got to stop this, she
thought angrily. I've got to stop this!

Matt and Mark came back from their trek a little
after six, and after they'd showered off the day's dust,
sweat and grime, they all sat down to dinner. Mark
was sitting opposite Sanny, pretending everything was
just wonderful, telling her about his day and the
things he had seen. He looked good, too good, in a
blue sports shirt that matched the colour of his eyes
and made his tan stand out. A lock of hair had fallen
across his forehead, giving his appearance something
boyish and carefree.

Tomorrow he would leave. Remember his voice, some hidden part of her said. Remember the sound of his laugh. Remember his eyes and the way he looked at you when you made love. Remember the feel of him, his touch, his kisses.

Why don't I get emotional about it? she asked herself derisively. Why don't I get sentimental and melodramatic and burst into tears right in front of everybody?

The food stuck in her throat and she nearly choked. She couldn't eat. She felt sick. His eyes were on her and she stared at her plate, feeling herself grow hot and cold in turns. Her hand holding the fork felt clammy. Putting the fork down, she got up from the table.

'Excuse me,' she said in a perfectly nice, controlled voice, and left the room. In the bathroom she splashed cold water over her face and hands. Why was she shaking? There was absolutely nothing wrong with her physically. Nerves, like some Victorian heroine. Maybe I'll even get the vapours and faint, she thought. A good thing nobody'd see me, because I haven't any idea how to do that gracefully. I'd probably hit my head on the sink and end up with a concussion.

'Oh, God,' she moaned, feeling hot tears sliding down her face, 'I can't stand this. I can't stand looking at him and thinking about him. . . .' Bending over the sink, she splashed more water on her face, then sat on the edge of the bathtub and dried off. Walking through the hallway to her room, she heard voices and the sound of knives and forks touching plates and serving bowls. She wasn't going back in there. But if she didn't somebody might come looking for her. Well, she'd cross that bridge when she got to it.

She got to it real fast. Only a couple of moments after she'd stretched out on the bed, breathing deeply and calmly and giving herself a lecture on the necessity of self-preservation, came a knock on the door.

'Just a minute!' She stumbled to her feet, took a deep breath and smiled as she opened the door.

Mark, grave and grim.

'Just coming out,' said Sanny, slipping past him into the hallway.

'Not so fast!' He grabbed her arm and pulled her back into the room and closed the door behind them. 'What was wrong with you?'

'Wrong?' She looked at him in wide-eyed innocence. 'Nothing was wrong. I needed to blow my nose, and I didn't have a tissue.'

'Nice try. Nobody stays away ten minutes to get a tissue. You looked ill. Are you feeling all right?' His eyes bored into hers. She stared straight back.

'I'm perfectly fine, thank you. Shall we go back?' She had no choice but to make that suggestion. Her pulse was still up, but she had things under control—she had herself under control. She'd clamped down on her emotions, forced herself to be cool and composed and it seemed to be working. 'I'm hungry for some dessert. Kwesi made some mango mousse. I bet it's delicious.' She smiled sunnily.

He scrutinised her for a moment, his face hard and angry. He seemed about to say something when he apparently changed his mind and turned away from her to open the door.

Sanny swept past him, feeling almost faint with relief. He'd looked as if he'd been ready to thrash her. Not that she really believed he'd ever lay a finger on her in anger, but even the threat of it was quite disconcerting.

The table had been cleared in their absence and the dessert was served as soon as they sat down.

'I heard a great joke the other day,' said Sanny. 'A

sheik was riding on a camel through the desert when . . . .'

It worked, it always worked. Matt had his head thrown back, laughing hard, and Jackie was holding on to her stomach. Only Mark wasn't amused. He glared at her across the table with so much cold anger that she felt a shiver go down her spine.

Next morning Mark swung his duffel bag in the back of Matt's car, hugged Jackie and wished her all the best with the baby, then turned to Sanny to say his farewells.

His face was expressionless as he bent and pecked her on the cheek. 'Goodbye, Sanny, good luck.'

'Have a good trip,' she said nicely, feeling like a block of ice inside, frozen, dead. Their eyes met for an infinitesimal moment, then he swung away and lowered himself into the car seat. Matt started the engine and the Peugeot slowly crunched down the gravelled drive and into the street. One last wave and they were gone. Goodbye, Mark—goodbye, love.

How she managed to get through the next few days, Sanny had no idea. It seemed as if somebody had taken over her mind and body and did her thinking and moving for her. It was an odd feeling to have everything go so automatically, as if she were merely a machine following orders: eat, sleep, work—whatever was appropriate at a given time.

Matt invited her to come along with him on a couple of his day trips and she visited his projects, one of which was located in a small village that sported a distinguished-looking village chief and a traditional medicine man. She interviewed both of them, which was an enlightening experience. The village chief, a regal old man with a grey beard, sat ramrod-straight on a stool of elaborately carved white wood. A large *adinkra* cloth printed with traditional symbols was loosely wrapped around his body and flung over one shoulder. He had a lot to tell her—about social and economic issues, about education, about his family of two wives and sixteen children, one of whom was in England on a goverment scholarship studying to be an engineer.

Sanny was sitting on a straight-backed chair opposite him in the shade of one of the mud buildings of the chief's compound. On the other side two women were pounding yam or cassava in a large mortar. She watched the rhythmic movements for a moment as she listened to the chief, hoping ungraciously that she wouldn't be invited to join them in eating the *fufu*. The starchy, doughy balls of pounded tubers were rather tasteless, but heavy like cement in the stomach, as she had discovered on previous occasions.

Not much later Matt appeared and the chief gave some orders in Twi, and soon they were offered calabashes of palm wine, a sparkling, sweet drink that Sanny found delicious. On entering the village that morning she had seen some people in the process of extracting the sap from the trunk of a large coconut palm. It was this sap, slightly fermented, which they were drinking now. It didn't keep well, Matt had explained, since it kept right on fermenting and in a few hours was a vile and potent alcoholic brew.

The medicine man, whom she interviewed later that day, was a jolly old man with a great sense of humour, which was not exactly the picture of medicine men she'd carried around in her imagination. She'd expected to find someone scary, secretive and sinister, casting satanic spells on innocent people.

This particular specimen looked like everybody's favourite uncle (give or take a little skin pigment), which however didn't mean that he did not take his profession seriously. He did, very. And so did the rest of the village, apparently. He explained to Sanny how he cured illnesses and saved lives by the use of herbal potions, magic brews and spiritual intervention. He seemed to have a generally benevolent attitude, which was reassuring, she had to admit.

Although Sanny did not consider herself superstitious in the traditional meaning of the word, she had decided that there were certain forces roaming the earth that had as yet not been explained by science. Some people were blessed (or cursed, depending on your outlook) with extra-sensory perception and had psychic powers which had been proved to exist, if not explained. Medicine men were probably part of this élite and used these powers in a manner appropriate to their cultural setting. As for the herbs, modern science was beginning to recognise the medicinal benefits of many herbs and plants—so no mystery there in Sanny's mind.

Back at the house she worked like a machine under remote control, typing away the hours on Jackie's portable typewriter, talking to Kwesi while he was cooking meals, talking to his wife, and coming up with all sorts of interesting material.

It was in the minutes before falling asleep that her true self seemed to emerge from all the frantic activity of her mind and body, and thoughts of Mark would take over. She dreamed of him every night for an entire week. Apparently she could force herself not to think about him in her waking hours, but in sleep her mind was beyond her control. The dreams were different every night—sometimes he was angry, sometimes loving and tender, sometimes indifferent like a polite stranger. . . .

'Don't you remember me? I'm Sanny!'

He frowned. 'I'm sorry, I. . . .'

'You've got to remember me! We spent two days

and two nights at the beach together! Don't you remember?'

He shook his head, looking apologetic. He was wearing shorts and no shirt and his hair was bleached white from the sun. She wanted to throw herself against his chest and hold him, but the indifferent look in the cool blue eyes kept her from it. And then she saw it. Suddenly it was there: a big tattoo on his chest. It was the shape of a red heart with an arrow going right through it and on one end it had an M and on the other an S.

Her heart leaped almost out of her chest. 'See?' she said, pointing at the tattoo. 'I'm on your chest! The S that's me! The S is for Sanny!'

'You're very confused,' he said calmly. 'I've never seen you in my life. Why don't you lie down for a while?'

Tears were streaming down her cheeks and she grabbed his arm. 'But what about the S? There's an S on your chest!'

There was amusement in his eyes now. 'That's for Sue. She's over there, the tall blonde with the blue eyes.'

'No! No! No!'

'I'm going to marry her. We're going to have a traditional ceremony with drummers and dancers, and the village chief will marry us.'

'You can't! I love you! You said you were never going to leave me! You promised! You promised!'

She woke up crying, struggling with the rumpled sheet that had got itself wound all around her like a cocoon. She disentangled herself from it, then stretched out and tried to relax.

Mark had never promised her anything. Why was she having these bizarre dreams? Mark with a tattoo on his chest—good grief! Mark who said he didn't know her— that was bad. She closed her eyes. I want some milk, she thought. A nice glass of cold milk.

Two days later Matt had to go to Kumasi for

business, his last trip out of town until after the baby
was born. Sanny decided to pack up and go with him
and travel north from there. She said her thank-yous
and her goodbyes to Jackie and wished her all the best
with the birth of the baby, almost wishing she could
stay on for the great event, but knowing she couldn't.

For the next three days she bussed and hitched her
way through lush green Ghana, feeling more alone and
more lonely than she had for a long time. She envied
Matt and Jackie their marital bliss, their excitement
over their baby. By comparison her life seemed empty
and cold. Was she going to be alone for the rest of her
life? Or was she going to settle for some cool and
comfortable relationship without emotional ties, one
that wouldn't destroy her if ever it broke up? She
thought again of Laurie and her engineer husband
living in a Liberian mining town and her blood ran
cold. She thought again of all the times she'd attached
herself to someone and the inevitable break-up after.
Love was not for her, Sanny Joy Copeland, not love of
any sort.

Having ferried across the Volta Lake and travelled
through the towns of Tamale, Navrongo and
Bolgatanga, she was approaching the border town of
Paga. The northern part of the country was dusty and
dry, and sitting in the cab of an ancient truck Sanny
surveyed the depressing landscape shimmering in the
heat. Huge, dead-looking baobab trees stood like
symbols in the dry soil. Here and there she noticed
egrets in the fields, graceful, slender birds—a pure
beauty in the dreary countryside.

But there were signs of work in progress. New huts
were being built—smooth round walls standing in the
fields waiting for roofs. Regular, low ridges in the soil
indicated the cultivation of peanuts, little hills that of
yams. The driver, a talkative Ghanaian with a friendly
grin and a magnificent set of teeth, explained all this to

her. He also told her about his family and about his mother-in-law who had loaned him the money to buy the truck. He hauled anything and everything, and he loved the road and the freedom and the travel. His philosophy of life had been put into two slogans painted on the truck. In front it said: TRAVEL AND SEE, and on the back it read: HAPPINESS IS THE SOUL OF LIFE. He was a happy man, he told Sanny. He had a good woman, three children and his own lorry. God had blessed him lavishly.

It was reassuring to hear about some bliss in the middle of all this bleakness, Sanny thought morosely, looking out of the cab window.

The bordergate was in the shape of an enormous Ashanti stool with a black star and the words BYEBYE SAFE JOURNEY on top. Weary and stiff, she jumped out of the cab and proceeded to drag her luggage out and into the concrete block Customs building. It didn't take her long to go through the formalities. Nobody showed geat interest in her or her belongings, and with her passport duly stamped she moved out into the hot sunshine again and walked through the gates and out of Ghana.

On the Upper Volta side of the border, a few hundred yards further, was a small establishment called 'Union Bar'—a few garishly painted buildings with a gravel courtyard that sported some chairs and Formica tables. Sanny decided to have a drink and wait for a while. There was no way of telling how long it would take the truck to pass through Customs, but she was in no great hurry.

She sat down at one of the tables in the shade of a gigantic baobab tree and ordered a mysterious soft drink by the name of Youki soda. *Aux extraits de fruits*, it said on the bottle. What fruits, she had no idea. It was a beautiful reddish orange, it tasted sweet, and it did the job of quenching her thirst. Back in French

West Africa, she thought, as she read the label. It all seemed so artificial. A few hundred yards down the road everything was in English. You crossed one artificial line and suddenly everything was French.

She felt quite comfortable sitting in the shade. The heat was drier here and not nearly as debilitating as the humidity of the coastal regions farther south. It was peaceful and quiet, with only the sounds of some scrawny chickens wandering through the courtyard pecking around in search of sustenance, and the buzzing of some insects here and there. The sky was an endless blue. Upper Volta—more dusty, dry stubble. What am I doing here? Sanny asked herself, feeling depression swamp her again. I could have been in Nigeria with Mark. Will I ever stop thinking about him?

She tucked a stray curl behind her ear and shifted in her chair. She felt dull and sad and listless all the time. The fun had gone out of her adventures. She wished Mark was here with her in this shady courtyard, drinking Youki soda, talking. She wished she could tell him some silly joke and see his impossible smile light up his eyes. She wished. . . . Oh God, she thought, stop this madness! Finishing the drink, she got up and looked at the wares displayed in the little shop attached to the bar—sweaters, cloth, gaudy Chinese thermos bottles, salad oil, cans of Dutch margarine, cheese, flip-flops.

A goat came wandering around the corner of the building, paying no attention to her at all. Fifteen minutes later Sanny was relieved to see the lorry coming to a stop. The driver called for her through the open window, grinning. He'd been lucky, he said, as she climbed into the cab. Nobody had given him any trouble. The road was good, he went on, and it would only be a few hours now and they'd be in Ouagadougou.

Dry savannah stretched out endlessly, with occasional clusters of huts, some people walking by the road here and there seemingly coming from nowhere and going to nowhere. Twenty miles or so out of Ouagadougou a big sign stood by the road in the barren wasteland. OUAGADOUGOU GOLF COURSE, it read. Sanny had to look twice before she believed her eyes. *Who* in this semi-desert played golf? The expatriate community in the capital? How did they get grass to grow? There was no green in sight.

There were a lot of people by the road now, many with donkeys heavily laden with enormous loads of firewood.

As dusk fell they arrived in Ouagadougou, a sprawling, dusty town with low buildings and streets full of cars, mopeds, donkeys, bicycles and hordes of people on their way home from work.

Giving profuse thanks for the ride, Sanny said goodbye to the driver, who grinned happily and said it had been his pleasure, that he hoped she'd had a pleasant time in his country and that soon she'd come back.

She had the names and addresses of a couple of hotels, one of them the Hotel de l'Indépendence, which was *the* place in town, with a superb French restaurant and a beautiful swimming pool. Obviously, this was not for her. With the help of a taxi driver she found one of the lesser establishments, a small place near the big market on the corner of a street. It was run by a French couple, the female partner of whom was sitting in the restaurant drinking wine and gabbing with a blonde friend who was decked out fit to kill with loads of make-up and high heels. A brightly coloured parrot sat on the bar, making disgusting noises.

Sanny was shown to her room, which was adequate enough with its own bathroom, a shower behind a curtain and a sink. She took a leisurely shower, feeling some of the weariness wash down the drain along with the day's accumulation of gritty dust. She felt ravenous, having only eaten fruit during the day, and her body craved some nourishment.

The Frenchwoman was still sitting in the restaurant drinking wine and talking to her friend. It was seven-thirty and probably too early for a civilised French dinner, but Sanny didn't care. She ordered veal stuffed with ham and cheese which turned out to be truly delicious. She enjoyed every bite, watching the other guests coming in as she ate.

She went to bed early, slept like a rock and dreamlessly for the first time in two weeks. Next morning, after a French breakfast of milky coffee and croissants, she made her tour of the town, checked in at the Consulate where she found a letter waiting from her editor, and came back to the hotel as dark set in. She took the key, but found the door unlocked. Going in, she stopped dead in her tracks.

Sprawled out on the bed, and sound asleep, lay Mark.

CHAPTER EIGHT

IT was a dream. It had to be a dream. Without making a sound Sanny put down the bag that held the few purchases she had made at the local market that afternoon and tiptoed closer to the bed. Mark looked calm and peaceful, the square chin relaxed in sleep. A blond lock of hair lay across his forehead, pale against the tan. Her heart hammered hard and loud, her stomach tightened nervously.

This couldn't be true. She was having another one of those bizarre, nightmarish adventures. In a moment he would sit up and grin at her and take off his shirt. She'd see the red heart tattoo and he would point at the S and say it stood for Sue, who was a very tall cheerleader whom he was going to marry. But if she, Sanny, loved him too, he'd marry her as well. He could become a village chief and have sixteen children, or maybe he'd become a fetish priest and they'd all live together happily ever after right here in Africa. They were already building the huts for their compound and they could move in as soon as the roofs were on.

She closed her eyes and opened them again a moment later. He was still there. She looked around the room, taking in the cheap flowered curtains, the worn linoleum on the floor, the wobbly table near the window. This was her room all right. A pair of her sandals lay near the chair. The paperback novel she'd been reading lay on the floor next to the bed with the same blue and red cover it had had last night. Her eyes moved back to the bed and the long body stretched out on it. Lightweight khaki pants, a green and blue striped shirt, bare feet. His sandals were on the floor.

Her eyes went back to his face and his eyes were open, studying her. Her heart leaped in her throat. She'd never felt like this in her life before—hate and love and pure panic and ecstatic joy all in one.

Why had he done this to her? Why was he following her around? She wanted to forget him. There was no place for him in her life. Oh, God, why had he had to come back? Why was it so silent in the room? Why didn't he say something?

'Hello, Sanny,' he said.

She stared at him, not answering his greeting.

'I happened to be passing through,' he explained casually, lips faintly smiling. 'I thought I'd look you up.'

Happened to be passing through. Nice try. 'How did you find me?' she asked. 'How did you get in?'

'I've been waiting around for the last two days. I checked at the Consulate this afternoon—they were very helpful. Downstairs I told them I'm your husband and I wanted to surprise you. You know the French, they love romantic intrigue. I had no trouble getting them to open the door for me.'

Closing her eyes, Sanny turned away from him. 'Why?' Her hands clenched by her side. 'Why are you here?'

She heard the creaking of the bed, and then he was behind her, hands on her shoulders. His touch sent a shock of emotion through her and she stiffened in defence. He pulled her close and she felt the warmth of him against her back.

'Because I want to be with you,' he said quietly. 'In Nigeria I had a lot of time to think. I thought about you a lot. I missed you very much.'

She felt like a limp rag doll. There was no feeling in her legs, no strength anywhere in her body. All she was aware of was the anguished longing for him—for his touching and loving. He could go away for a thousand years and it would be like this when he returned. It would always be like this. He was in her blood, and there was no weapon she knew of that could fight the attraction he held for her. It was everything—his voice, his laughter, the look in his eyes, the curve of his mouth, the shiny fair hair falling over his forehead. There was something indestructible between them.

Science should find a cure for this sort of debilitating condition, she thought numbly. A permanent inoculation or some purple pill to be taken with a glass of hot milk before retiring at night.

She steeled herself, straining against him. 'I-want-you-to-let-me-go. I-want-you-to-get-out-of-my-room.' Her jaws felt as if they were set in concrete.

He made not a move, stirred not a muscle. 'I'm not leaving. At least not until we've had a good talk. I want you to tell me a few of your stories.' He sounded determined, paternal and domineering, which enraged her.

'I don't have to tell you anything!' she exploded. 'I told you I didn't want you to follow me around any more! I hate you! I want you to leave me alone!' She pushed and pulled, quite ineffectually, at the hands encircling her waist.

'And no hysterics, please,' said Mark, unperturbed. He turned her around so she faced him and before she could say another word, his mouth closed over hers. He kissed her forcefully, holding her body in a steely grip.

Hot anger flared, then faded. Where words had failed, his kisses succeeded. The long-smouldering fire inside her burst into flames, melting resistance, consuming thought and reason.

How long they stood there, she had no idea. He muttered something unintelligible, then withdrew and took her hand, pulling her towards the bed. She looked at him in a daze.

'No,' she whispered. 'No!'

'Sanny, we've got to talk,' he said quietly. He sat down heavily and the bed creaked ominously under his weight. He pulled her down next to him and as she sagged down a dreadful crash rent the silence, and she fell against him as the bed collapsed beneath them.

For a moment neither one moved or spoke. They lay sprawled across the caved-in bed in the most awkward position, Sanny draped half over him and half off the bed. She felt his body begin to shake, then heard the sound of deep rumbling laughter. He rolled around holding her in his arms, and there was another splintering sound and something else gave way and the lower end of the mattress sank to the floor. Mark had her pinned underneath him now, looking down into her face with stars of merriment in his eyes.

'This could only happen to you,' he said, grinning crookedly.

'You've got it. Now let go of me, please!' She squirmed beneath him, which was not a smart thing to do, as she realised immediately. He bent his head to hers and began to kiss her. It was a deeply sensual kiss that quickly became more passionate and unconstrained until he broke away unexpectedly. He came to his feet, pulling her with him. Sanny leaned against him, trembling. She wanted him desperately, her treacherous body taking no notice of the warnings of her mind. She pressed her face against the green and blue striped shirt, hearing the dull thud of his heart. It was beating fast, as fast as her own.

'Sanny,' he whispered, 'come with me to my hotel. We can have dinner there; we can talk.'

And make love and sleep in each other's arms and wake up together. No, she thought. Not again.

'No.' She took a deep breath and straightened away from him. 'I'm staying right here. Why don't we have dinner downstairs? The food is really good. I'll tell them about the bed and maybe they can do something about it while we eat, or give me another room, or something.'

'Maybe. They may decide that you and your husband are too wild and passionate for their furniture.' He grinned devilishly.

Sanny groaned. 'Oh well, I don't care.'

He bent down to inspect the bed, lifting the mattress and looking underneath. The mattress had been supported by wooden slats that had succumbed to old age and improper construction. 'Actually,' he said, 'I don't believe we're the first to go through this contraption. Don't feel too bad.'

'I wasn't feeling bad.' She watched as he dropped the mattress and straightened himself to his full length. He looked strong and virile and she felt weak with longing. 'Before I go down,' she said in her calmest voice, 'I want to get out of these clothes and into the shower, and I don't want you in here while I'm doing that.'

There was unconcealed amusement in his eyes. 'I'll go down and have a drink. I'll wait for you in the bar.' He opened the door and strode out. Sanny stared after him. She hadn't thought it would be so easy to get rid of him.

She stripped off her clothes, stepped in the shower and closed the flowered curtain. After a day like today, having cruised through the open market and the dusty streets in the blistering heat, she considered a shower the highlight of her day. She turned on the taps.

Nothing. No water. Not a single drop.

'This can't be happening to me,' she said out loud. 'I refuse to believe it.' She twiddled with the taps. Nothing.

'Believe it,' she muttered angrily. 'You have no water.'

She stepped from behind the shower curtain and marched to the sink and tried the taps. No water there either. She glared at her reflection in the mirror.

'You might as well face it,' she said to herself, 'there is no way you're going to get a shower.'

'This body needs one.'

'What had you expected? This isn't the Hilton or the Holiday Inn. This is a family place in an African town on the edge of the Sahara. Water might be a precious commodity in a place like this.'

Sanny turned away from herself. She didn't feel like being reasonable. Not while she was tired and dirty and sticky. Maybe *after* a shower she could be reasonable and realistic, but not before one.

I'm not going to climb into my precious clean clothes, she thought furiously. Putting back on the clothes she'd tramped through town with all day wasn't particularly appealing, either, but she did it anyway. She was going to complain downstairs. Not that she had any great hopes that complaining was going to accomplish any miracles and make the water flow from the taps, but it might make her feel better. Maybe. She groaned in frustration as she swung out the door. Complaining in French wasn't easy. Complaining was best done fast and fluently, using just the right words, and she wasn't going to pull that off in a foreign language. She might as well forget it.

In her best, politest French she mentioned the fact of the lack of water, which apparently was no great shock to the proprietor. 'Maybe tomorrow,' he said congenially.

Maybe not, she thought nastily.

Mark was in the bar having a drink. He looked at her with raised eyebrows. 'I thought you wanted to take a shower,' he remarked.

'I did, only there's no water. That made it rather a difficult undertaking, so I gave up.' She sank down on a bar stool next to him.

'Water is always a problem in a town like this,' he said with total lack of surprise.

'I suppose I could buy a couple of bottles of Perrier and pour them over me.'

He nodded agreement. 'You could. I had a friend

who once travelled through some remote place and the only wet stuff around was Coca-Cola. He washed his hands in it.'

'Sounds delicious. May I have a drink, please? Like a double Scotch, so I can anaesthetise myself and forget my troubles.'

'I have a better idea. Pack up your things and come back with me to my hotel, have a shower, a drink by the side of the pool, then dinner.' He looked at her calmly.

It was the best offer she'd had all day, all year, in all of her life.

'No, thanks,' she said, giving him her sweetest smile. 'Why does your hotel have water and mine doesn't?'

'A matter of economics, I'm sure.' He looked at her with faint exasperation. 'Don't be silly, Sanny. There are two single beds in my room. I have one, you take the other.'

'Easy and simple,' she said sarcastically.

He shook his head. 'Not so easy, not so simple, but it's your choice.'

She took a deep breath. 'All right, you win.' She slid off the stool and without looking at him she rushed out the bar and back to her room. She threw her clothes into her suitcase and slammed it shut just as Mark walked into the room.

'Ready?'

'Yes.' It didn't sound very friendly.

'What's the matter now?' He was leaning lazily against the doorpost, watching her with a frown.

'Nothing is wrong! Except for a collapsed bed and no water, that is. And now this!'

'Now what?'

She glared at him. 'Going with you to your hotel, which I assume is the sumptuous Hotel de l'Indépendence, is going to be the stupidest mistake I've ever made in my life! And I *know* that! And I'm still *doing* it! And I can't *stand* myself for being such a moron!'

The silence was short but heavy. 'Don't fight it,' he said at last.

'Easy for you to say!' She closed her eyes for a moment and sighed. 'I'm sorry, forget I said anything. Let's go, I'm looking forward to that shower.'

In the taxi she began to babble cheerfully about her day, the sights she had seen, the mysterious wares in some of the market stalls—rocks and powders and potions and pastes, the people she had met and talked to.

'I'll get you a room of your own,' he said as they entered the spacious, plant-filled lobby. 'Then you won't have to worry about a thing.'

'No! I mean, absolutely NO!' She grabbed his arm. 'I'll walk right out of here if you do!' She couldn't afford one herself, but no way was she having him pay for her. 'I'll share yours. Just lead the way.'

He gave her a long hard look. Then he took her elbow. 'Come along, then.'

The shower was a delight. She dressed in her best dress, which was the same long, floating affair she'd worn before, sprayed on a liberal dose of Jungle Jasmine perfume and did the best job ever on her make-up. This was only for her own benefit, of course. She wanted to feel clean and cool and gorgeous because it was good for her self-confidence and morale. It didn't matter what Mark thought about the way she looked. She grimaced at herself in the mirror. 'So, and who do you think you're fooling?' she said to her mirror image.

They had drinks and a long leisurely dinner, French style, with several courses and lots of wine and sophisticated French waiters who looked like penguins in their evening clothes.

'There still seem to be a lot of French people

around owning and running things here,' she said. 'I thought the colonial days were over.'

'They are, but the French did things differently than the British.' He gave her a true professorial smile. 'The French still have quite a bit of economic control over their former colonies, for various reasons.' He elaborated on this point for a while and Sanny listened while she slowly ate her ice cream dessert, asking a question now and then. Going out to dinner with a professor of economics could be an educational experience. No harm in learning a few things here and there, and as long as she could keep him talking about impersonal subjects, she wouldn't have to worry about what to say or what to do.

After they arrived in his room later that night, he made no efforts to be more personal. He offered her the use of the bathroom first and she got ready for bed and slid in between the sheets. Then he did the same, getting into the other bed, wearing nothing.

'Goodnight, Sanny,' he said, switching off the bedside lamp.

'Goodnight. And thanks. This bed is great.'

'Good.'

Silence.

Was she disappointed? Of course not. She was relieved. She thought of him lying in the next bed wearing nothing. He hadn't even kissed her goodnight. She closed her eyes, remembering the feel of his mouth and the touches of his hands and the warmth of his body against hers. Of all the things she could be doing right now (say her prayers, count sheep, think about her work, sleep, and so on), this was not the most productive. She could lie here and make herself good and miserable in two minutes flat. She could get up and go over to his bed and say, please make love to me because I can't stand this any more. I love you, please love me back.

She turned around with a sigh and tried to think of something else. The bed was very comfortable. The sheets were cool. The central air-conditioning was working beautifully.

'Sanny?'

'Mmm . . . what?' Her heart began to gallop.

'Do you have the feeling that maybe something isn't quite right here?' There was a smile in his voice.

'Everything is just perfect. The bed, the sheets, the air-conditioner. This is truly Paradise.'

'And I'm Adam and you're Eve.'

'Oh, for heaven's sake! You have only one thing on your mind!' Not that he was the only one. . . .

She heard him laugh. 'Don't you find this situation slightly ridiculous?'

'Not in the least.'

'Do you know how boring Nigeria was without you?'

'No.'

'Very, very boring.'

'I'm sorry.'

Silence. 'Do you think you'll be able to sleep?' he said then.

'I'm sleeping now.'

'Of course, how dumb of me. Did you ever go to summer camp, when you were a kid?'

'Yes.'

'And sit around a fire and tell ghost stories?'

'Yes. Do you believe in ghosts?'

'Absolutely,' he said.

'I know a good ghost story. You want me to tell you?'

'Is it scary?'

'Very, very scary.'

'Okay, tell me.'

She did. In a very low, hushed voice. It was truly a hair-raising tale, at least if you were six years old, one she remembered from years and years ago. It had terrified her senseless. But she'd been a child then, and now, somehow, it was more funny than anything else. She did her very best, getting carried away with all the sinister, bloodcurdling details, until suddenly she nearly jumped out of her skin when she felt something touch her arm.

'It's only me,' said Mark, and before she knew what had happened, he'd slid into bed with her.

'Get out of my bed!'

'I just got in.' He snuggled close to her, smothering a laugh. 'It's your own fault. You terrified me with that story. I'm afraid all alone in bed.'

'I'll bet!'

His body was shaking with silent laughter, and he began to kiss her neck.

'I hate you!' she whispered fiercely.

'I know just how you feel. It's hell, isn't it?'

Sanny struggled against him, against herself. 'You're mean and devious. You're a damned sex maniac!'

'I know. It's a cross I have to bear.'

She couldn't stand this any longer—he was setting her on fire with his kisses and sensual caresses and the movements of his body. She gritted her teeth, making herself rigid.

'Mark, stop it! I mean it!'

Surprisingly, he did. He looked down into her eyes. 'Why?'

'Because I don't want to make love!'

'Why not?'

'Because I'm tired, I have a headache and you'd mess up my hair!'

He shook his head disapprovingly. 'No good. Come up with something more creative.'

'I don't want a cheap fling with you.'

'All right. How about an honourable, discreet affair?'

'No!'

'Have any thoughts about marriage?'

'None whatsoever.' She pushed at his chest to no avail. First thing she was going to do when she got back home was take up judo or ju-jitsu or maybe karate.

'About marriage in general or about marriage to me?'

How was she going to keep cool and calm with his body pressed against her? How could she stay unmoved by their closeness when everything inside her cried out for him?

'My thoughts about marriage in general are negative and not worth noting,' she said levelly. 'My thoughts about marriage to you are non-existent.' Oh, if only she had the strength to push him out of bed!

'Don't you ever want to get married? Not even to me?' He pretended to look surprised and wounded.

'Not even to Prince Charming himself. Now get out!'

He didn't He lowered his head and put his cheek against hers, very gently and for a moment he lay very still, not moving.

'Sanny,' he said then in a suddenly deep and husky voice, 'I want to make love to you so badly, it's driving me crazy.'

There were a number of smart remarks she could make in answer to that, only she was incapable of uttering a sound. She wanted him, longed for him with a raw intensity she couldn't fight. She loved him even though it filled her with terror.

His lips moved across her cheek. 'I keep remembering that night at the beach. Every damned night since then I've dreamed about you. What happened, Sanny? What happened after that? Why did you change your mind?'

Because I panicked, she thought, not wanting to remember, not wanting to think and talk any more. She lay silent, listening to the pounding of her heart, feeling the weakness of her limbs.

'Sanny . . . tell me you don't want me and I'll leave.'
His voice sounded strange.

She opened her mouth, but not a sound came out.
She shook her head helplessly and closed her eyes,
putting her arms around him. She didn't care any
more. Nothing mattered.

In the morning it mattered very much. She heard him
whistling in the shower when she woke up, sunlight
streaming across her face. A cold rage filled her. How
could she have let this happen to her? Listen to him!
Listen to those triumphant sounds coming from the
bathroom! He had done it, hadn't he? He had very
successfully seduced her! She wouldn't be surprised if
the catastrophes of the crashing bed and the lack of
water had been staged by him to get her into his hotel
room.

She jumped out of bed, picking up the nightgown
that lay discarded on the floor and slipping it back over
her head. The bathroom door opened and Mark came
out, bringing in with him a waft of soap and shampoo.
He was drying his hair with a towel and another one
was wrapped around his waist. His eyes were warm
and smiling as he looked at her.

'Good morning, angel.'

Angel! She felt like the devil himself, like a mean
vicious, fire-spewing dragon—green, spiky, ugly.

He moved towards her, dropping the towel over a
chair. His hair stood out in wet peaks and he looked
ridiculous. He reached for her and she backed away.

'Don't touch me!'

Surprise sparked in his eyes. 'What do you mean,
don't touch me? What's going on here?' He took her
shoulders and studied her.

She gritted her teeth. 'I said don't touch me,
because I don't want you to touch me!'

'Good God, what's the matter with you? Are we

going to start this ridiculous routine all over again?'

'Let me go.' Her voice sounded low and shaky, and he scrutinised her with amazement.

'Sanny, for God's sake, what's the matter with you?'

'I hate you,' she whispered. 'You make me do things I don't want to do. You make me think things I don't want to think! You make me feel things I don't want to feel! You. . . .'

'I think I'm beginning to understand,' he said slowly. 'You don't hate me, Sanny, and you know it. You hate all those ghosts in your past who hurt you and disappointed you—your father, your tattoo Peter, and, God knows, your mother too.'

'You know nothing about it, so don't give me that!' She'd never told him anything about her mother, the alcoholic; about the way she'd grown up, shuttled from one family to another, giving her love because she needed to love and be loved; about the pain of loss and rejection. He knew nothing about any of that.

'I know enough. I understand a few things without you having to spell them out for me. I also know about myself and my own feelings for you. I know I want you with me. I know I love you.'

'Yeah, that's what they all say,' she said sarcastically.

Mark's face grew taut and something flickered in his eyes. 'Sanny,' he said in a low voice, 'don't you talk to me that way.'

'I'll talk to you any damned way I please!' Her legs were shaking, suddenly. She wrenched her shoulders free from his grip. 'You say you love me—well, I'm sorry, it doesn't mean a thing to me! Not a damned thing!' She ran into the bathroom, locked the door, turned on the water taps, flushed the toilet, turned on the shower and burst into uncontrollable weeping. Sitting on the edge of the tub, getting drenched by the spray of the shower, she cried her heart out.

'Sanny, open the door!' He shook the door handle, his voice hard and angry. She didn't bother to answer, couldn't have made a sound, anyway. Getting to her feet, she pulled off the soaked nightgown and got under the shower while the tears kept flowing freely.

He loved her, he'd said. Well, it didn't mean anything, did it? He wasn't the first to say that to her. He wasn't the first who had wanted to marry her for that matter, either. Peter had loved her, and he'd married someone else. Her mother had loved her, but hadn't been able to take care of her. All the 'aunts' and 'uncles' had loved her, and they'd all disappeared out of her life one way or another. Why would Mark be any different? He'd find somebody else, or he'd get tired of her, or change his mind or . . . there were any number of reasons, and she knew them all. Laurie had been madly in love with her Swedish husband and now she hated him with a passion and he was fooling around with someone else. Within her group of friends, colleagues and acquaintances she could count a dozen divorces and a number of miserable marriages. Love. It didn't mean a thing.

So, she said to herself, why then do you feel so wretched?

There was a horrendous crash and the sound of splintering wood, startling her so she almost slipped. My God, she thought in horror, he's broken down the door! The next moment he was next to her in the shower, water streaming down his face, towel still around him. He drew her wet body against his and kissed her hard on the mouth.

'I love you,' he said, 'and it'd better mean something to you, because I'm not giving up until it does. I don't care what you tell me—I love you.' There was no laughter in his eyes, and his mouth was grim.

'For how long?' Sanny heard the raw pain in her own voice.

'For ever, Sanny. For always.' Not a moment's hesitation in his voice, not a flicker in the steady regard.

That's what you say now, she answered in bitter silence. She closed her eyes against the water streaming down her face. Words, only words. So easy to say, so easy to forget.

'You don't even know me,' she said dully. 'You know nothing about me.'

'Feelings are sometimes more important than facts.' His lips brushed hers and he kissed her slowly, but she stood unmoving in his arms. Something slid down between their legs—the waterlogged towel giving in to gravity. Mark seemed oblivious to everything except her, holding her with a possessiveness she would have found irritating in any other man.

It was happening again. He was doing it to her again. Her senses were stirring in dizzying delight. There was nothing more sensuous than the feel of his smooth, wet body touching hers, the strong hands sliding down her back, the warm water flowing all over them as they stood together, holding, touching. . . .

She tried to fight the feelings in desperate denial, but her hands moved on their own and her lips began to respond to his. It was all so hopeless, so utterly hopeless.

'Sanny,' he whispered against her mouth, 'will you marry me?'

CHAPTER NINE

THE water was no longer coming down. Had he turned off the taps? Hands wiped wet hair out of her face.

'Answer me, Sanny. Will you marry me?'

Sanny opened her eyes and looked at him. 'No,' she said in a voice so cool and clear and confident, it couldn't possibly be her own. 'Of course not.'

'Of course not?'

She stepped back a little and looked straight at him, unwavering. Strength and determination came flooding back. 'You're suffering from a temporary derangement, Professor. Africa does that to people sometimes. The heat, the dust. . . .'

His face gave nothing away. 'When are you ever going to be serious, Sanny Joy Copeland?'

Her smile was devastating. 'I'm deadly serious. Marriage is out for me. Later you'll thank your lucky stars.'

'Later, *you* may be sorry,' Mark suggested with a charming smile of his own.

'Not a chance. I know what's best for this little girl, and marriage isn't it. I know myself too well.' She had to get out of there and get her clothes on. Standing naked in the shower next to an equally naked man wasn't what she needed right now.

'I doubt it.'

'Be my guest.' She turned and stepped out of the shower, and he let her go. Taking a dry towel, she left the bathroom, dried off in the bedroom and dressed in record time. He came out as she was packing her things away.

He dressed swiftly, saying not a word, then started

throwing clothes and shoes in a suitcase too. She was done first, slung her handbag over her shoulder, picked up her bag and made for the door.

'Wait a minute,' he ordered. 'I'll go down with you and have breakfast.'

'I don't want any, thank you.' Her courage and control were slipping away. She wanted to get away from him as fast and as far as possible before she'd do something she'd regret for the rest of her life ... before she'd turn and throw herself in his arms and tell him she loved him and wanted to marry him and live happily ever after. She clung to a shred of sanity which told her there were no happily-ever-afters for her. Life didn't have those in store for her, Sanny Joy Copeland. She'd learned the hard way.

'We can be civilised about this, can't we? The fact that I asked you to marry me and that you said no isn't the end of the world, you know.' He was smiling reassuringly, as if she were the one who had been turned down and needed comfort.

'I'm glad you can look at it that way. I was afraid I might have crushed your precious male ego.'

'Not a chance,' he quoted. 'I'll just keep on asking.' Still that impossible grin, those irresistible eyes. She fought the weakening of her heart.

'You have a lot of courage,' she mocked.

'Whatever it takes to get you. Don't imagine for a moment that you're going to get rid of me.'

Strangely, having said that, after he had eaten breakfast with the appetite of a coal miner, he had left for the airport and got on a plane for Paris.

Sanny felt abandoned, deserted—which was so ludicrous she began to doubt her own sanity. Had she expected him to stay here and pursue her through the Sahara? She didn't want him to, did she? Apparently he was a lot smarter than she was. At least he had the insight that she wasn't in any state of mind to make life-changing decisions. He was going to leave her alone. For the time being.

He doesn't even know my address, she thought suddenly, staring vacantly at the splintered doorpost of the bathroom. Well, a little thing like that wouldn't keep him from finding her. He'd been successfully chasing her all over West Africa, certainly he'd have no problem at all doing it in the United States of America.

And while she was sorting herself out here, coming to her senses, as he no doubt expected she would, he was going to enjoy himself in Paris. Deflated, she stared at the bathroom door.

She could stay in the room, he'd remarked casually. It had been paid for for two more days and the damaged door would be taken care of. Vaguely she wondered what he had told the hotel manager.

She didn't stay; she couldn't. She wanted to get away. This whole situation seemed to take on the characteristics of a nightmare. Nothing made sense— not her own feelings, not Mark's actions. What did he want with her, a waif, a stray?

That night she found herself in a large mud hut village with the long name of Fada Ngourma, somewhere in the middle of nowhere on the road to Niamey, Niger. It had a gas station, a school, a church, a clinic, an open market, and a *campement* where she stayed the night in a dusty room lying awake on a faded pink and yellow sheet that looked none too clean.

She had arrived in the early afternoon, and had been unable to find a ride to take her further east to Niamey. Fada was an attractive place with wide, unpaved lanes lined with trees and low, neat mud houses. There was no electricity. She had explored the village and the open market, admiring the traditional shirts and wool blankets.

After a dinner of roast chicken, which was really dry and incredibly tough guinea hen cooked too long over a charcoal fire, Sanny sat down outside for a while, enjoying the cool night air and listening to the shrieks of bats in the trees and the sounds of drumming coming from somewhere in the village.

It was not only the lumpy bed and her uneasy thoughts that kept her from sleeping that night. She lay awake listening to the drumming that continued all through the night until the early hours of the morning. It stopped as sunlight filtered into the room, and for a while she slept, dreaming restlessly.

'I can always ask again,' said Mark.

'It's absurd. I wouldn't marry you if you were Prince Charming himself.'

They were standing, fully dressed, he in a pin-striped suit, she in a slinky silk dress, under the shower. It was the shower in her bathroom at home with its sea-green tiles, hanging plants, and softly glowing light-bulbs surrounding the mirror.

'Do you love me?' he asked.

'No.'

'Why not? I'm handsome and charming and a professor of economics and all my female students want to marry me.'

'Why then don't you marry all your female students and have a harem? You'd like that, wouldn't you?'

'Only if you were my Number One wife.'

'I don't like harem pants and veils, and *couscous* is fattening.'

He began to take off her clothes and suddenly they were somewhere else, on a tropical beach with palm trees and foamy waves splashing at their feet.

'This is Paradise,' he said. 'And I'm Adam and you're Eve.'

'Adam never wore a pin-striped suit,' she said disdainfully. 'You're a fraud.'

'So are you. You pretend you don't love me.'

'I don't. I don't know how to love. I've never really learned how. My mother left me when I was four years old and she never loved me, so I didn't learn.'

'You are your own person,' he told her. 'Your mother belongs in the past. Don't blame her—she has no influence over what you do now.'

'I hate you! You know nothing about it! Nothing, nothing, nothing!'

'You don't hate me.'

'I do! I do! I do!'

She struggled out of sleep and burst into tears.

Rain and wind and falling leaves—yellow, orange, red and brown. Autumn. November. Warm skirts and wool sweaters, hot chocolate, apple pie, beef stew. Sanny found relief and comfort in being back in familiar surroundings, in her own apartment with its sea-green bathroom, minuscule kitchen, the Indian rug, her books, her own comfortable bed, her own coffee cup, her very own electric typewriter.

Strangely, her very own typewriter didn't do nearly as well as some of the foreign contraptions she'd used in Africa, ones that had some keys in different places and some not at all and some extra. Maybe it was the fact that her brain refused to function. She couldn't think properly any more—not about the book and the columns she still owed to the paper. Looking through her notes and reading about her African experiences brought back feelings and thoughts she didn't want to remember. She had hoped that time and place would create some sort of alienating distance between the then and now, but it hadn't. Sitting solitarily here in her apartment with the wind lashing the windows was the present reality, but it faded away as soon as she began to read and write, and she was back on the palm-shaded beach in the tropics with a man with blue eyes next to her in the sand, asking her about the tattoo on her thigh. She felt his hand on her leg again, heard the sound of his voice as if he were next to her in the room talking to her. Raising her head, she looked around the room just to make sure. He wasn't there.

She began to wonder if she needed to do something drastic and soul-destroying in order to purge herself from the memories—such as tear up all her notes and forget the book, forget her hopes of an independent professional life. She'd have to go back to the *Chronicle* and write about other people's weddings and the citizens of the week who'd done Great Deeds and made the world A Better Place in Which to Live.

She didn't want to write about other people's honourable actions; she wanted to write about her own adventures. After all, that was why she had taken the courageous leap into West Africa—so she would have stories to tell. Stories about rubber plantations and happy-go-lucky missionaries and market mammies and medicine men and camels. Camels she'd seen in Niamey, Niger, where her trip had ended—camels with heavy loads swaggering through the streets right along with the trucks and the cars and the motorcycles. It had been quite a sight.

Niger was different from all the other places she had seen, being mostly sand and desert. Niamey, the capital, was a sprawling town, sandy and colourless in the blinding sunlight. She'd met up with a couple of Dutch volunteers who had taken her into the desert and shown her what miracles could be wrought with water and money and knowledge and hard work. The desert could bloom, truly. The luscious green of a sea of sugar cane had not been a mirage.

They had introduced her to an American who for years had been involved in disaster relief work and he'd told her horror stories of the terrible drought, of

large trucks dumping grain in the desert and starved
women sifting through the sand to catch every last
kernel; of women who tried to push their babies
through his car window for him to take away and save
from starvation.

Eating a delicious meal in—of all places—a
Vietnamese restaurant, he had told her that and more.
It had been a depressing conclusion to her stay in
Africa, as she was due to catch a plane to Paris the
next day. Still, this was all part of the total picture and
Sanny had written it up dutifully, describing Africa as
a place of contrasts with wealth and power, poverty
and helplessness. With fancy hotels and mud hut
villages and beautiful villas and medicine men and
western-trained doctors and imported cheese and
apples and champagne and undernourished children.
She'd seen a little of everything, eaten a little of
everything, stayed and slept in places of all sorts, met
people of all kinds. It had broadened her vision and
enlightened her mind, and she would never be the
same again.

'I'll never be the same again,' she whispered to
herself, seeing Mark in her mind's eye, seeing every
line of his face, the shape of his nose, the colour of his
eyes, the twist of his smiling mouth. Something had
happened to her when he had appeared at the
Monrovia party and come into her life.

Sanny had never thought she would be able to love
again. She had fought against it for so long, she'd
imagined herself to be immune.

I'm never going to write this blasted book, she
thought in desperation, staring at the typewriter in
front of her. The empty page glared at her accusingly.
What I need is a party, people—something.

When a phone call came the next day with the deep
voice of some old flame inviting her to a feast of
magnificent proportions with live music and wine and

food and many wonderful people, she knew her prayer had been answered.

She appeared at the party fully decked out in her finest (slinky black dress slit to the thigh, high-heeled strappy sandals), face made up to perfection and glossy curls coifed beautifully. She felt reborn. This was the good life. Women looked at her enviously, men lustfully. She still had most of her deep tan, making everybody else look pasty as bread dough by comparison.

'So, how's Africa?' enquired another one of her old flames. He was tall, handsome, but not too bright. Kindness and generosity made up for some of that, but not all. Once she had broken his heart.

'It depends,' she said mysteriously, sipping delicately from her wine.

'On what?'

'The time and the place. And how are you?'

'Oh, I'm doing well.' He began to elaborate on exactly how well he was, giving full details about his appendectomy, his new car, and his personal discovery of an excellent Roumanian wine. Sipping California wine and looking interested, Sanny waited anxiously for an opportunity to escape, which presented itself shortly and smiling ravishingly, she disappeared.

Fortunately not everybody was as boring as poor Freddie and it was nice to see so many of her friends again. She laughed and joked and danced the night away, revelling in all the attention and admiration. Apparently not everybody had expected to see her return from Africa alive. Some seemed to find it surprising, if not disappointing, that she hadn't contracted some exotic disease. Possibilities were suggested all around—cholera, typhoid, yellow fever, sleeping sickness. In that department, however, Sanny had nothing to report, not even a bout of malaria.

'They have injections these days,' she informed them mildly, 'and weekly prophylactics for malaria.'

The discussion changed to wild animals. She had nothing to report on personal experiences in that area, either. No snakebites, no encounters with crocodiles and baboons.

The discussion took on a sense of the absurd for Sanny. It had nothing to do with her experiences. She wasn't sure how she would present to them the reality of her adventures, and she decided that now was not the time or the place. She'd write her book and give them each a nicely autographed copy to read.

She whirled her way through more parties after that, went out with old friends, and some new, and found herself spending more time in front of the mirror than in front of the typewriter. She was acting loose and irresponsible and living frivolously. For weeks she hadn't done anything, written not a single page, spending her days in bed and her nights on the hunting trail. She wanted a man, an interesting man who would take away some of the emptiness that seemed to balloon inside her. A man who would fill her up with laughter, but who would leave her deeper emotions alone. She couldn't find one.

One night, after she had come back from some lavish affair where she had eaten too much and drunk too much and laughed too much, she scrutinised herself in the mirror, seeing her seductive clothes and the warpaint on her face and a cold realisation swept over her.

'You're a fraud, Sanny Joy Copeland,' she told herself brutally. 'And you've been one for a very long time.'

After that she didn't go to any parties any more, not to movies or dinners or other gatherings. She stayed home and ate frozen dinners in front of the television. She started writing again because she had no choice.

Her finances were in sorry shape and if she didn't start producing she'd be dining on dog food in a few months. Freezing out feelings and memories (and taking tranquillisers so she wouldn't succumb to the strain of it) she began to work on her book again. Most of the material was already written, but it needed a good working-over and some changes here and there.

For three weeks she worked like a machine, going out only to do laundry and grocery shopping and to go to the library and post office. She had Christmas dinner with a friend and for the rest managed to ignore the entire season, locked up in her room. Christmas was a depressing time—it had always been. Having no family to go home to, she usually spent the time with friends who were equally lonely and equally depressed.

In the middle of February—she'd been home three months—she heard from Mark. A business envelope arrived in the mail containing an open airline ticket to Madison, Wisconsin. It was a one-way ticket. No return.

The shock of it shattered the frozen isolation of her feelings. There was no letter, but on the jacket of the ticket he'd scrawled *I love you—for ever*.

She hadn't expected to hear from him again. She had given up the secret hope weeks ago, assuming he would come to his senses once back in his natural habitat of university and swooning students. He must have realised his demented thinking in wanting to marry her, she had concluded, telling herself how very relieved she was.

Obviously, she had been wrong.

All night she sat up, staring at the ticket and the *I love you—for ever*, remembering. Remembering everything. She awoke into a grey morning with fog floating past the window, her head on her arms on the kitchen table, chilled to the bone.

Her half-eaten dinner of a cold, gooey, once warmed-up frozen pizza (15–18 min. at 400 degrees, the carton said) stared her in the face. All around her lay the debris of a day gone by: dirty coffee cups, half a glass of souring milk, wilting plants that looked at her accusingly, a sloppy stack of newspapers on the floor, shoes she'd kicked off the night before, a magazine with some gorgeous female on the cover— eyes like stars, sparkling teeth, blossoming cheeks, ripe lips, hair like dark silk ... it was a depressing sight. She felt cold like the pizza and wilted like the plants, and she probably looked the colour of a baked potato, and she resented the glowing face on the magazine cover.

Stiffly she got up, groaning as her body complained with every movement. In a small saucepan she heated some milk and drank it standing up, slouched against the kitchen counter. Then she struggled into her bedroom and out of her clothes, leaving them where they dropped, and crawled under the covers. After a while the combined heat of the milk and the fluffy comforter warmed her through, and she sank deep into sleep, and Mark was there telling her he loved her and would never leave her because without her life would be so boring.

It was almost ten when she woke up again and the fog was still clouding the window. The apartment was frigid like a meat locker. She turned up the thermostat, made some coffee and toast and got back into bed, robe and all, taking the magazine with the glowing model on the cover with her. She ignored the sections on fashion and beauty and health and settled for an article that told the story of a couple of campers who'd got mauled by brown bears in the Rocky Mountains and had lost various arms and legs between them, but had survived. It cheered her up considerably. Who said *she* had problems?

Today she should make good use of her arms and legs and clean up the apartment before she lost herself in the clutter. She fried herself two eggs and had more coffee and toast. Then, dressed in jeans and shirt, she set to work.

First on the list was picking up the assorted debris of her unorganised lifestyle. The ticket she put away in the bottom of her underwear drawer, underneath the silky pinks and mauves and burgundys and honeys of her slips and bras and panties. Why she put it there, she had no idea. It seemed a safe, private place. She stripped the bed of its flowered sheets and remade it with white ones she hadn't used for ages, and they looked very strange—pure and virginal and very old-fashioned. Now, she thought, surprised, why did I do that? She stared at the chaste, maidenly bed for a full minute, then shrugged. There were a lot of things she didn't understand. Over this one she wasn't going to lose sleep.

She went into a rage of cleaning, dusting and vacuuming, keeping up a running dialogue with her Other Self, discussing and arguing about what to do with her life if her book was a flop, what to do about the ticket to Madison, Wisconsin, and what to fix herself for dinner that night. With the zeal of a crusader she emptied closets and cabinets, wiping and washing and scrubbing and sorting through three years of accumulated possessions cluttering the closets. Spring-cleaning in February—she had to be demented.

In a cardboard box stored away in the corner of her wardrobe she found the blue notebook. Her heart began to thud heavily. Her hands shook as she opened the cover and recognised the childish handwriting, round, irregular, uncertain. Eight years old she'd been when she'd started the journal. Before her were the pages of the collected miseries, pain and loneliness of her childhood. It had been years since she had last seen these notebooks.

Not wanting to, but irresistibly drawn, Sanny began to read, feeling herself eight years old again, lonely and frightened and worried about Daddy David.

Surrounded by dusting cloth, spray cleaner, scouring powder, a bucket of dirty water, soap and paper towels, she read and wept. 'Oh, Mama,' she whispered, 'why didn't you let me go? Why didn't you love me enough to give me up? I'd have a family now—parents, brothers and sisters maybe—a place to belong. I'd have a place to go home to, a mother and father to talk to and tell my troubles to. Maybe if I'd had all that I wouldn't be so terrified of that ticket in my underwear drawer. . . .'

She dreamed again that night and the night after that, and each dream was more bizarre than the others, all mixed up with the people and the places from her book, on which she kept working feverishly. One thing the dreams had in common: Mark kept chasing her and asking her to marry him, and each time she said no.

'I don't want to marry you! I don't, I don't, I don't!' She was running through the sand, scrambling to get away, but there was no place to hide. There was nothing but sand. Sand until the horizon. Sand left and right. Sand in her hair and nose and ears and mouth.

He was chasing her across the desert sitting on a camel wearing flowing white robes and a piece of cloth wrapped around his head like an Arab. There was something very strange about that, and her mind struggled with that while her legs made their tortuous moves through the hot sand. This was Black Africa, West Africa. There weren't supposed to be any sheiks around here.

Mark caught up with her and she felt herself swept up into his arms and deposited in front of him on the camel. He held his arm firmly around her waist and whispered in her ear that he was taking her to his *casbah* where his harem had planned a big welcoming party for her. He had an accent as he spoke, but when she turned around to look at him he was really Mark, with royal blue eyes and a princely smile.

The casbah looked just like the Hotel de l'Indépendence in Ouagadougou. He parked the camel between a blue Citroën and a yellow Peugeot, and then suddenly they were back in the bathroom where he took off her clothes and turned on the shower for her. The white robes were gone and he was wearing a towel which he left on as he stepped under the shower with her.

In the bedroom a party was in progress. Through the open door Sanny could see a lot of people, among whom were several beautiful young girls, who were his students, and Jackie and Matt and the Dutch volunteers chewing sugar cane. The village chief, wearing his *adinkra* cloth, was standing on the table eating a banana, and the medicine man was sprinkling white powder on Jackie's feet.

'Sanny Joy Copeland,' said Mark, looking very solemn, 'will you marry me?'

'No, of course not!' She got out of the shower, hurried into the room, dripping water and wearing nothing, and the medicine man turned and looked at her gravely.

'You are a very unhappy person,' he said, and everybody was suddenly very quiet, listening to his words, which he repeated once more. He then began to sprinkle the white powder on her head and shoulders. Suddenly it was coming down in a great cloud, covering her whole body until she was completely white and looked like a ghostly apparition and everybody ran screaming from the room, except Mark.

By now she was crying hysterically, and he picked her up in his arms and took her back into the shower. The water was warm and comforting, his hands gentle and careful as he began to wash off the powder with handsful of foamy soap that smelled like vanilla. She began to feel extremely light, almost as if she were floating, and a great happiness filled her. Delirious with sweet sensation, she smiled at Mark, and then he lifted her up again and carried her to the bed and began to make love to her.

'You'll be happy for ever after,' he said, 'the medicine man promised.'

And Sanny knew it was true.

Until she woke up.

She wondered if her dreams would stop if she ever said 'yes' and agreed to marry Mark in her dreams. But in her dreams she might never say yes, and she'd go on having those ludicrous nocturnal adventures for the rest of her life.

Something needed to be done. Never before had she lost sleep over any man, except Peter, but he was her first love and she'd not known any better.

Thinking about Mark, thinking about actually marrying him, made her break out in a cold sweat. Fear paralysed normal thought and she felt herself give in to hysterical emotions about the fear of rejection and abandonment. But the ticket in her drawer kept haunting her, and a decision needed to be made.

The ticket, and all it symbolised, was on her mind all the time, like the weight of a ton of gravel. She thought about the other ticket, torn in two in the wastebasket in the Simmons' house. It made her think of Matt and Jackie who had by now had their baby and were the delighted parents of a son. She'd received in the mail a birth announcement proclaiming joy and gratitude at the birth, and stating sex, height and weight of the baby.

Maybe she should have confided in Jackie, Sanny thought, and asked her about the secrets of a successful marriage and a happy life. More and more these days Sanny began to feel the need to talk to someone, to unburden herself, to lean on somebody. It was a frightening development, because she'd stood alone for many years now, not needing anyone.

The days felt heavy with the threat of a pending decision: to tear it up, or not to tear it up. She felt filled with doom and gloom, and a darkening fear. In her drawer lay the ticket to Madison, waiting quietly, patiently. She tried not to touch it when she was in the drawer taking out clothes, as if it were some venomous insect hiding in the dark among her slips and bras, ready to sting. In her mind it seemed to have grown into a living thing with tentacles and stingers and fangs.

It was absurd, she decided in one of her more lucid, saner moments. She wasn't going to let herself go crazy over this any longer.

The next day she took a plane to Madison, Wisconsin.

The apartment door opened and Mark's blue eyes looked down at her without surprise.

'Well, hello there,' he said smoothly, as if he'd been expecting her at just that moment. Well, maybe he had, Sanny thought. Maybe he was psychic and had known all along that she would be coming.

'Hi!' She beamed him one of her best smiles, her heart jumping up into her throat.

'Welcome to Wisconsin.' He was sportily dressed in tight-fitting jeans, a plaid shirt and a leather waistcoat, and he looked disgustingly fit and healthy. What had she expected? To find him thin and emaciated from lack of food and sleep due to worry over her?

'Always wanted to visit Wisconsin,' she said brightly. 'I heard the cheese is very good here.'

'So are the apples,' he mocked. 'Why don't you come in and have some?'

It was like a movie with a bad script, she thought as she stepped inside on to the honey-coloured carpeting. She'd had several visions as to how this meeting would take place, had even rehearsed entire sentences, speeches, lengthy confessions and unburdenings of the heart in preparation. At one of the mental rehearsals Mark had been speechless with joy to see her, pressed her against his heart and kissed her senseless. At another, she herself had been so overcome with emotion, she had broken into tears at the sight of him. Cheese and apples, however, had not figured in any of her imagined dramas.

He closed the door behind her, turned to her, hands on his hips, and gave her a close look. A crooked little smile played around his lips, but his eyes were hard to read.

'You made it,' he said softly.

Sanny began to peel off layers of clothing—scarf, hat, gloves, coat, extra sweater. 'What had you expected?' she commented evenly.

'I was beginning to think I'd have to change tactics and shanghai you.' He took her coat and assorted items and put them away in the hall closet. 'I was considering paying you a visit.'

'Mark. . . .' Why did she feel so utterly helpless? She wished she could think of the right words to say, but she had no idea what the right words were. She had no idea at all what to do next. 'I . . . I'm not sure I did the right thing in coming here. I'm not sure about anything . . . I . . .'

'My God,' he said softly, 'you're shaking!'

It was true, she thought in horror. She was trembling all over. 'It's nothing,' she said breezily, 'I'm only slightly terrified, that's all.' She watched him, seeing the expression change, the smile vanish. He expelled a long breath and then she was in his arms and he was holding her tightly. 'Sanny,' he murmured, 'what am I going to do with you? How am I going to make you trust me?' And then he wasn't talking any more, but kissing her with a fierce hunger that sent shock waves all the way through her. Her body blazed into life and for a few rapturous moments the world faded away. Nothing had changed in those last three months, nothing at all. She loved him and she would never love anyone else.

The realisation terrified her. Had she secretly hoped her feelings for him would have changed? Disappeared? Had she hoped secretly she would feel nothing when she saw him again so she could feel safe once more? She wanted safety and peace badly. She'd wanted it so much ever since she had come back from Africa, but it had eluded her. Mark had followed her in her dreams and there had been no solitude, no safety.

'Sit down,' he said huskily, letting her go and guiding her to a chair. 'Have you eaten? Are you hungry?' He looked grim.

'I had plastic beans and rubber chicken on the plane. I'd like a glass of milk, though.'

'And some Alka Seltzer?' he suggested with a faint smile.

'No, thanks. My stomach is used to abuse. I've been feeding it TV dinners lately.'

She took a quick look around her as he left her to get the milk. It was an attractive apartment. The living room was done in muted browns and creams with touches of blue. The couch and chairs were comfortable. There was a wall full of books, a fireplace and several exotic pieces of art decorated the walls and bookcase. Some she recognised as African, others seemed more oriental in origin. She sauntered over to the direction in which Mark had gone and found the kitchen where he was busy mixing himself a drink. The milk stood on the counter.

'Are you sure you don't want something else?' he asked.

'Nothing, thanks.'

There was a strange tension between them, an intense awareness of each other. It was hard to look at him without feeling an odd prickling sensation going through her. She shivered lightly.

'Would you mind if I heated the milk?'

'I wouldn't mind,' he said with a touch of humour in his voice. 'What is it with you and your obsession for milk? Anybody else in your position would be bolting down the booze.'

She shrugged. 'I had a friend once who took psychology and he had it all worked out. He said it had to do with lack of nurturing in early childhood. He said milk for me is like a security blanket.' She manufactured a careless smile. 'So you see, it's all my mother's fault. Don't blame me.'

Mark rolled his eyes. 'He sounds brilliant. It's amazing how many eighteen-year-old Freuds there are. I trust he's now enjoying the great future that was ahead of him then.' He poured the glass of milk into a saucepan and put in on the stove.

'He left college after his first year. Last I heard he was training sled dogs in Alaska.'

He laughed, a wonderful deep sound. Sanny shivered again, not knowing why.

'Are you cold?'

She shook her head, feeling silly. 'No.'

'Nervous?'

'Of course,' she grinned. 'That's why I want milk.'

He raised his eyebrows. 'So you think your friend was right?'

She shrugged. 'I wouldn't be surprised. I had a lousy childhood. My mother was an alcoholic and they took me away from her when I was four.' She had her eyes fixed on the toaster and wild panic surged through her. *Shut up!* she said to herself. *Shut up!*

'Then what?' he asked, cool as spring grass.

'Then what nothing.' She picked up the saucepan. 'This must be hot by now.' She poured the milk back into the glass.

She was amazed at her own capacity for chit-chat. Drinking her milk, she watched him across the table, and chattered about everything and nothing until the tension became unbearable. The strength to say another word failed her, and she lapsed into silence. Staring at her hands, clasped nervously in front of her on the table, she wondered if she was going to crack up any moment now.

'Sanny?'

'Yes?' She didn't look up.

'I love you.'

She swallowed. 'I love you too,' she whispered. She had said it, finally said it, and it was worse than she'd thought it would be. Terror gripped her, choking her. She couldn't breathe, *she couldn't breathe!* Covering her face with her hands, she gasped and then some terrible sound escaped her.

'Sanny!' she felt herself being pulled out of the chair and into Mark's arms. Pressing her face against his chest, she broke out in a storm of weeping.

'Sanny! For God's sake what's wrong? What's the matter?'

'I can't . . . I can't stand this! I can't. . . .'

'Can't stand what?' He sounded perplexed.

'I love you . . . you say you love me . . . what . . . what am I going to do when it's over?' Every word was a struggle. She gulped and forced herself to go on. 'What . . . am I going to do after you leave me? How long is this going to last?'

He stepped back and lifted her face. 'What the hell are you talking about? Who says I'm leaving?' He looked almost angry.

'There's an end to everything, isn't there?' She sounded bitter, but some of her composure had returned, if only a little. 'I'm afraid I don't have a lot of romantic illusions. The people I love never stay around—they move on to better things. It's always been that way, it's the story of my life.' She took a deep shuddering breath and disengaged herself from his grasp. 'Why would it be any different this time? Why would you be any different from any of the others?' Her voice had suddenly risen, and she heard the sound of pain reflected in it, felt the memories sweep over her full force. *'Why would you be any different from the others?'* she repeated with anguished despair. She wiped tears away with her hands and saw him standing there, staring at her, his face white.

'Sanny,' he said after a terrible silence, 'I asked you to *marry* me! How much more permanent can I get?'

'Marriages break up—people are unfaithful! People fall out of love. *Nothing* is permanent!'

'Sanny, not all marriages break up. Not all people are unfaithful, and not all people fall out of love. My parents have been married for forty years and they're still very much in love.'

'Well, *mine* didn't manage more than a few months! My mother took to the bottle, and I ended up in foster-homes, one after the other, and nobody . . . nobody. . . .' Her voice broke and she turned her back on him, fighting tears.

They were on the couch, she didn't know how she'd got there, and the words came pouring out. With a flood of tears she told him everything, all the pain and rejection and loneliness of her childhood, the longing for a family, a permanent home, people who would always be there, who would love her without reservation.

Mark listened to her without speaking, his arms around her. She lay against him with her eyes closed, unable to look at him while she spoke. It was like a purge, an exercise in exorcism. Everything that she had hidden behind her armour of smiles and laughs and jokes lay now exposed and bare between them.

'I'm scared,' she said at last. 'I think of loving you, of being married to you, and it terrifies me. I can't help it. If it would end, I couldn't take it. I couldn't take it one more time.'

'Then why did you come to me?'

'I had to. That ticket . . . that stupid ticket was haunting me. I couldn't tear it up.' She managed a watery smile. 'And I was dreaming about you all the time. You wouldn't believe how absurd and bizarre those dreams were. You were always after me and I couldn't stand it any longer. I had to straighten myself out, one way or another. I had to come and find out what my feelings really were.'

She withdrew from him and came to her feet. Standing away from him, hugging herself, she studied his face. 'I keep asking myself what's the matter with me. Am I demented? Deranged? Unbalanced? All of the above?' She grimaced, laughing a little. 'What do you want with me, anyway?'

Mark stood up too, but didn't come over to her. Hands in his pockets, feet slightly apart, he scrutinised her. 'You *know* what I want with you. I want to marry you, but not until you feel safe and secure enough. We'll have to work on that, won't we?'

'I don't know how.'

'We'll have to find a way. If you love me enough, it will all work out.'

'You sound so confident,' she said miserably. 'How can you know? How can you be so sure?'

He came over to her then, putting his hands on her shoulders and looking deep into her eyes. 'Sanny,' he said quietly, emphatically, 'besides all the obvious aspects of love—the infatuation, the attraction, the feelings of closeness and belonging—besides all that, Sanny, love is a decision.'

The words seemed to echo in the silence. *Love is a decision.* She had never heard that one. She looked into his eyes, not knowing what to say, saying nothing.

'That's what keeps it going in the long run, through bad time and difficult situation,' Mark said softly. 'Love isn't just something you feel, some state of mind you have no control over. Love needs nurturing to stay alive, and that is a conscious decision every day, Sanny. It expresses itself in all the little daily things that happen between people.' His hands slid down her back and he drew her closer. 'Love doesn't just stop or fly out the window. It dies from neglect.' He paused. 'Sanny,' he continued softly, 'I love you. My promise to you is that I will not neglect that love.'

She swallowed at the constriction in her throat. A joyful peace was settling inside her. 'I love you too,' she whispered. 'And I need you, I need you so very much, Mark. Please help me.' Her face was pressed against his chest and she felt his arms tightening around her.

'We'll have to help each other,' he said quietly. 'Together we can do it all.'

Strength filled her, and the growing conviction that with Mark she could give herself one more chance— one last chance at love. She would need time, maybe a lot of time, before she would really feel free of her fear. It wouldn't just vanish overnight.

He lifted her face to his and smiled. 'Remember in Africa you used to say "I have stories to tell"? The stories I wanted to hear you wouldn't tell me. You were such a little phoney, hiding behind your brave little smiles and your silly little jokes.'

'And still you fell in love with me?'

'You weren't hiding well enough. You were actually quite transparent, only you weren't aware of it.'

'Now you know everything. I've told you all my stories.' Sanny felt overwhelmed with relief. She'd be all right if she could learn to trust and have faith in the strength of their love. It felt right to be here in his arms, to touch him and tell him she loved him. He was strong and loving and understanding, and with him she would be safe.

She felt his hand slide under her sweater, felt the tenseness of his body and the rapid beat of his heart.

'Sanny,' he murmured against her lips, 'we've talked enough for a while, don't you think?'

'Yes,' she whispered, feeling warm and lightheaded and full of love and longing. She met his eyes and smiled. 'Why don't you show me the rest of the apartment?'

Mark laughed softly. 'All right. Let's start with the bedroom.'

Harlequin® Plus

A WORD ABOUT THE AUTHOR

Karen van der Zee is an author on the move. She was born in Holland, studied in the United States and then married a man whose work, as an agricultural adviser in developing countries, has taken the family to such faraway places as Liberia and Ghana.

It was in Ghana, in fact, that Karen stumbled across a Harlequin romance for the first time—at a neighbor's home. Karen, who already had poetry and short stories published in Dutch, was now fluent in English. After reading her first Harlequin, she knew she wanted to expand into this field of writing.

The result of that desire was *Sweet Not Always* (Romance #2334), her first novel, set in the primitive jungle of Ghana.

Karen enjoys the opportunity of being able to introduce her readers to new places and cultures, and she would like to get to know her audience more personally. "You can say you write for yourself," she explains, "but that's not really true."

Karen, her husband, Gary, and their family make their permanent home in the United States. For most women a move to another country – or another continent – means pulling up roots. For Karen van der Zee it means a chance to discover a brand-new setting for a brand-new book.